Billionaires of London

Finding love in the world's greatest city!

Billionaire bachelors Hugh Moncrieff and
Roland Devereux might not be searching for
love, but when the Faraday sisters walk into
their lives they'll pay a price far greater than
their wealth to live happily-ever-after…
they'll lose their hearts.

Billionaire, Boss, Bridegroom…?

Meet gorgeous CEO Hugh Moncrieff
and the charming and quirky Bella Faraday
in this whirlwind office romance!

Available March 2016

and

look out for Roland and Grace's story

coming soon!

Dear Reader,

I love writing linked books. So when my editor asked if I'd like to write a duet about two sisters I jumped at the chance!

The Faraday sisters are total opposites—Grace is quiet and sensible and restrained, and Bella's a vibrant free spirit. But they love each other deeply, and when Bella gets the chance to be the sister who rescues, instead of being the one who's always rescued, she jumps at the chance.

And that in turn leads her to an encounter with a gorgeous stranger—who turns out to be her new boss! (Coincidence? Yes…) And when Hugh calls in the favour Bella ends up playing the role of his ditzy new girlfriend.

Except play-acting turns into something much more— and a chance to heal both Hugh's and Bella's heart. If they can overcome their differences…

If you like music (especially *The Sound of Music*), dogs, beautiful Elizabethan mansions and vibrant city life, I think you'll enjoy Bella and Hugh's story.

With love,

Kate Hardy

BILLIONAIRE, BOSS...
BRIDEGROOM?

BY
KATE HARDY

First published in Great Britain 2016
By Mills & Boon, an imprint of HarperCollins*Publishers*
1 London Bridge Street, London, SE1 9GF

Our policy is to use papers that are natural, renewable and recyclable products and made from wood grown in sustainable forests. The logging and manufacturing processes conform to the legal environmental regulations of the country of origin.

Printed and bound in Great Britain
by CPI Antony Rowe, Chippenham, Wiltshire

Kate Hardy always loved books and could read before she went to school. She discovered Mills & Boon books when she was twelve and decided this was what she wanted to do. When she isn't writing, Kate enjoys reading, cinema, ballroom dancing and the gym. You can contact her via her website: katehardy.com.

Books by Kate Hardy

Mills & Boon Romance

Behind the Film Star's Smile
Crown Prince, Pregnant Bride
A New Year Marriage Proposal
It Started at a Wedding...
Falling for Mr December

Visit the Author Profile page at
millsandboon.co.uk for more titles.

For Charlotte Mursell and Sheila Hodgson—
with love and thanks for letting me
have so much fun with this story. x

CHAPTER ONE

I'm coming to get you, Bella texted swiftly. *Hold on.*

For once, it looked as if she was going to be the res-
cuer instead of the rescuee. With her new job to boost her
confidence, she thought she might just be able to handle
it. For once she would be the sister who was calm, collected and totally together instead of the flaky, ditzy
one who always made a mess of things and needed to be
bailed out of a sticky situation.

She glanced around and saw a black cab waiting at the
kerbside. Relieved, she rushed up to it and jumped in.

'Can you take me to the Bramerton Hotel in Kensington, please?' she asked the cabbie.

There was a dry cough from beside her, and she
whipped her head round to discover that there was already a passenger sitting in the back seat.

She'd been so focused on getting to Grace that she
hadn't even noticed the other passenger when she'd
climbed into the taxi.

'I'm so sorry,' she said. 'I didn't mean to be rude.
Look, I realise that you were here first, and technically
I ought to leave right now and let you get on with your
journey, but I really do need to get to the Bramerton as
quickly as possible. Would you mind finding another taxi

and...and...?' She waved a desperate hand at him. 'Look, I'll pay for your cab.' It'd mean extending her overdraft yet again, but what were a few more pounds if it meant that she could return the favour for once and help Grace? Besides, she was about to start a new job. Next month, her cash-flow situation would be a bit better.

'Actually, I'm heading towards Kensington myself,' he said. 'I'll drop you off at the Bramerton.'

Relief flooded through Bella. She'd found the modern equivalent of a knight on a white charger: a man in a black cab. She wouldn't have to let her sister down. 'Thank you. Thank you so much.' She gave in to the impulse, leaned forward and kissed him soundly on the cheek. 'You have no idea how much I appreciate this.'

'What's so urgent?' he asked as the taxi drove off.

'It's a family thing,' she said. It wasn't her place to tell anyone about her sister's situation, let alone tell a complete stranger.

'Uh-huh.' He paused. 'Did I see you just come out of Insurgo Records?'

She looked at him, surprised. The man looked like a businessman on his way home from a late meeting, and he was hardly the target market for an independent record label—even though Insurgo's artists were a real mixture, from folk singer-songwriters to punk and indie bands, with a few oddities thrown in. 'Yes,' she said.

'Are you one of their acts?'

In her black jeans and matching plain T-shirt, teamed with a shiny platinum-blonde bob, Bella knew that she probably looked as much like an indie musician as she did a graphic designer. 'No,' she said.

But the man had been kind enough to let her share his taxi, so she didn't want to be rude to him. Besides, making small talk might distract her enough to stop her worrying about whatever had sent her normally cool and capable big sister into meltdown. She smiled at him. 'Actually, I'm a graphic designer, and I'm starting work at Insurgo next week.'

'Are you, now?'

Something about the way he drawled the words made alarm bells ring in the back of her head. But he was a total stranger. She was making something out of nothing. 'Yes, and I'm really looking forward to it,' she said with a bright smile. 'I'll be designing website graphics, album covers and band merch. Actually, I'm still trying to get my head round the fact that I've just been offered my dream job.' In an ideal world she would've preferred to have Insurgo as a client rather than as her employer, but working for someone full-time again meant that she'd have a regular income for a while—and right now she needed a regular income rather more than she needed her freedom.

'You don't know who I am, do you?' he asked.

'Other than a stranger who's been kind enough to let me share his taxi? No,' she admitted.

'Allow me to introduce myself,' he said, leaning forward out of the shadows and holding out his hand.

Bella caught her breath. He was gorgeous. Dark hair that was brushed back from his face, cornflower-blue eyes, and the kind of jawline that would've made him a hit in any perfume ad. She really had to resist the urge to reach out and trail her fingertips down his clean-shaven cheek. And that mouth. Almost pouting, the sexiest mouth she'd seen in a while.

Almost in a daze, she shook his hand, noting how firm his handshake was. And she studiously ignored the fact that her palm was tingling; after the way Kirk had let her down, she was officially off men. Even if this one was very easy on the eye and was wearing a beautifully cut designer suit, what looked like a handmade white shirt, a silk tie and highly polished Italian shoes.

No involvement.

Full stop.

Because she was never going to let anyone make her feel as foolish and useless as Kirk had made her feel, ever again.

'Hugh Moncrieff,' he said, and he waited for the penny to drop.

It took five seconds.

'Hugh Moncrieff—as in *Insurgo's* Hugh Moncrieff?' Bella asked in horror.

'That would be me,' he said. And he looked as if he was enjoying her reaction.

He was her new boss? 'But—you can't be.' Even though it would explain why he'd asked her if she was one of the artists; he must've thought that his second-in-command had signed her up in his absence.

'Why not?'

'Because you—you—' She gestured to his suit. 'You don't look like an indie record label owner. You look like a stockbroker.'

'The bank always likes the company's MD to wear a suit,' he said mildly. 'If I'd turned up to the meeting in ripped jeans and an avant-garde T-shirt, with funky hair, they'd have seen me as less of a professional and more of a risk.'

The bank? That nasty feeling got a lot worse. If he'd been to the bank for a meeting, all dressed up, at this time on a Friday evening, did that mean the company was in trouble and her job would be over before it had even started?

Her fears must've shown on her face, because he said, 'It's our annual review, and I went for a drink with a business contact afterwards. Don't look so worried. So you're my new graphic designer?'

'Bella Faraday,' she said. 'And I'm very good at what I do.'

'I expect you are, or Tarquin wouldn't have hired you,' he said dryly.

'So what are you doing in a taxi, when you own a record label? Why don't you have your own car, or a limo or something to drive you around?' The question was out before she could stop herself and she groaned inwardly. Way to go, Bella, she thought. Just grill your new boss, two minutes after you insulted him by saying he didn't look like the owner of an indie record label. Carry on like this and you'll be picking up your cards on Monday morning instead of starting your job.

So much for never letting herself feel foolish again. Right now she felt like a prize idiot.

'That's an easy one.' He smiled. 'My car happens to be in the local garage, having something fixed. I'd rather put my money into the business than waste it by hiring a flashy limo to do little more than wait around for me all day. Hence the taxi.'

Bella could feel the colour swishing through her cheeks. 'I'm sorry. It's not my place to question you. Look, um, please ask the cabbie to pull over and drop me off, and I'll get out of your way and find myself another taxi.'

'You said it was urgent—a family thing.'

'It is.'

'Then let me get you to the hotel. Tarquin obviously

overran with the interviews and made you late in the first place, so it's Insurgo's fault.'

'No, it's not,' she said. It wasn't anyone's fault. But right at that moment she was more worried about Grace than about making a good impression on her new boss, so she'd accept the offer. 'But thank you for the lift. I really appreciate this.'

'No problem.'

She texted Grace swiftly.

In taxi now. Wait for me in Reception.

Finally the taxi driver pulled up outside the Bramerton Hotel.

'Thank you again, Mr Moncrieff,' she said politely. 'How much do I owe you for the cab fare?'

'Nothing. You're practically on my way,' he said.

'Thank you. Really. And I'll work late every night next week to make up for it,' she said, and left the taxi before she could say anything else stupid.

When she walked into the reception area, Grace was waiting there, white-faced and silent. And there was no sign of Howard. Why wasn't Grace's fiancé waiting with her? Had something happened to Howard? No, of course not, or Grace would've said something in her texts. Not just that single word: Help, followed by rejecting Bella's call and sending a second text: Can't talk now. And now Bella was seriously worried. What on earth had happened?

But Grace had been right about one thing. They couldn't talk about it here. Not with Howard's parents' golden wedding anniversary going on in one of the function rooms. Whatever it was, Bella had her sister's back. And they were leaving. Now.

'Come on. Let's get out of here,' Bella said softly, put her arm round Grace and led her out of the hotel.

Back in the street, she looked around for a taxi.

Then she realised that the taxi that had dropped her off was still waiting at the kerb, exactly where she'd left it. And Hugh Moncrieff was still there too, though he'd moved seats so that his back was to the cabbie. He wound the window down and beckoned them over. 'Can I give you a lift somewhere?'

'But—' she began.

'Everything's clearly not OK,' he said softly, looking at Grace, 'so I'll drop you and…your sister, I presume?' At her nod, he continued, 'I'll drop you where you need to go. What's the address?'

Bella definitely didn't want to leave Grace alone tonight, and her own flat wasn't big enough for two. Biting her lip, she gave him Grace's address. 'Thank you so much,' she said. 'We both really appreciate this. Especially as you didn't have to wait.'

'No problem.'

She helped Grace into the car. Grace still hadn't said a word. Worried, Bella took her hand and squeezed it; but Grace didn't return the pressure. And this time nobody seemed disposed to make any small talk. With every second, Bella felt more and more awkward.

Then, just as the taxi turned into Grace's road, Grace threw up. All over Hugh's posh Italian shoes and suit trousers.

'I'm so sorry,' she mumbled.

She looked almost as mortified as Bella felt—and Bella had no idea what to say. What could you say when your sister threw up over your new boss? Apart from an equally apologetic, 'I'm so sorry.'

Hugh brushed it aside. 'These things happen. Do you need help getting her indoors?'

'Thank you, but no—I think you've done more than enough to help us, this evening.' Bella took a deep breath. 'Look, I'll pay for valeting the taxi and I'll pick up the bill for dry-cleaning your suit and replacing your shoes.'

'We'll sort it out later,' he said. 'Are you sure you can manage?'

'I'm sure,' Bella fibbed. At least she had Grace's spare door key, so actually getting into the flat wouldn't be a problem. 'And thank you. And sorry. And—'

'Just get your sister safely inside,' Hugh cut in. 'We'll sort out everything later.'

'Thank you. And I'm sorry,' Bella whispered again, and helped Grace out of the taxi.

This really wasn't how Hugh had expected to spend a Friday evening. Or how he'd expected to meet the newest member of his team.

The poor woman had looked horrified when her sister threw up everywhere.

Did Bella often rescue her sister like that? he wondered. Funny, the other woman had been dressed so soberly, in a navy linen dress and sensible shoes. Looking at them together, most people would've guessed that the younger woman was the one who partied too hard and would be most likely to throw up in the back of a taxi and need looking after.

Or maybe Bella's sister hadn't been drunk. Maybe

she'd been ill. But then surely Bella would've said that her sister was ill, or even called an ambulance?

But it was none of his business. He should just take a step back and ignore it.

'I'm sorry about all that,' he said to the driver. 'If you can drop me home, I'll pay for the cost of valeting the taxi and lost fares.' He gave the driver the address.

Though he still couldn't get Bella Faraday out of his head. Especially the moment when she'd kissed his cheek; it had felt as if he'd been galvanised. And then, when she'd shaken his hand, every nerve-end had been aware of the feel of her skin against his.

Hugh was definitely attracted to her. More attracted than he'd been towards anyone in a very long time.

But.

After the whole fiasco with Jessie, he'd learned his lesson well. Hugh would never, ever mix work and plea-sure again. As Tarquin had just hired Bella as their new graphic artist, it meant that she came firmly under the category of work. So he'd have to just ignore the pull of attraction in future and treat her just the same as he did every single one of his colleagues—by keeping her at a professional distance.

Even if she did have the sexiest mouth and sparkliest eyes he'd ever seen.

No involvement.

No risks.

This time, he'd stick to the rules.

'I'm so sorry I was sick everywhere,' Grace said once they were sitting down inside her flat.

Bella frowned. 'Didn't you eat anything to line your

stomach before you started knocking back whatever it was that made you throw up?'

'Champagne. No,' Grace said miserably. 'My stomach was tied in too many knots to eat.'

And Grace hardly ever drank. It wasn't a good combination. Not to mention really worrying—what had been so bad that Grace had had to get drunk? She took a deep breath. First things first. She needed to get Grace sober. 'Right. First of all you're having water—lots and lots of water,' Bella said. Then she looked through Grace's cupboards. Please let there be something that she could actually cook. Or, failing that, cereal to soak up all that champagne.

Then she spied the box of porridge oats. Perfect. Even she could follow the instructions on the box and make porridge in the microwave.

While the porridge was cooking, she took a banana from Grace's fruit bowl and chopped it up. She added it to the finished cereal and put the bowl in front of Grace, who immediately pushed it away.

'I can't.'

'Eat it,' Bella said firmly. 'Your electrolytes are all over the place and bananas are great for sorting that out, and oats will help because they're bland carbs which will raise your blood sugar without upsetting your stomach.'

'How do you know all this stuff?' Grace asked, looking bemused.

Bella smiled. 'Remember I dated a doctor a couple of years back? He gave me the lowdown on the best food to eat for a hangover.'

'I'm sorry,' Grace said again. 'Was the taxi driver very angry?'

'Don't worry,' Bella said airily. 'My boss is sorting it.'

Grace did a double-take. 'Your *boss*?'

'Uh-huh.' Bella flashed her sister a grin. 'Guess what? I got the job.'

'I—oh, my God. Are you telling me that I just threw up over your boss before you even started the job?' Grace asked, looking horrified as Bella's words sank in. 'Oh, no. I'll talk to him and explain, so he doesn't sack you or—'

'Gracie, it's fine,' Bella cut in.

'It's not fine at all! I've messed things up for you. Look. I'll pay for the dry-cleaning.'

Bella smiled. 'I already told him I'd do that, and I said I'd pay for valeting the taxi as well.'

'My mess, my bill,' Grace said. 'I'll pay.'

'Gracie, just shut up and eat your porridge. I don't want to hear another word from you, young lady, until that bowl is empty.'

'You sound like Mum,' Grace muttered.

'Good,' Bella retorted. Usually Grace was the one who sounded like their mother and Bella was the one hanging her head in shame.

She made Grace eat every scrap and drink two more glasses of water before she resumed her interrogation. 'Right. Now tell me—what happened?'

'I can't marry Howard.'

It was the last thing Bella had been expecting. Her older sister had been engaged for the last four years. OK, so Howard was a bit on the boring side, and his parents were nightmares—Bella had dubbed them Mr Toad and Mrs Concrete Hair with good reason—but if Grace loved him then Bella was prepared to be as sweet as she could to them. 'What? Why not? Don't you love him any more?' And then a nasty thought struck her. 'Is there someone else?'

'Of course there isn't anyone else.' Grace shook her head. 'I wouldn't do that to him.'

'Not deliberately, no, but you can't help who you fall in love with,' Bella said. She'd fallen for Mr Wrong enough times, and Kirk had shattered her trust for good. She'd never trust another man with her heart again, no matter how attractive he was. It had taken her six months to re-build her life—and she was still angry with herself for being so naïve and trusting. Why hadn't she been able to see that he was stringing her along?

'I love Howard, but I'm not in love with him,' Grace said. 'There's a difference.'

'I know.' Bella squeezed her hand. 'And it's a big dif-ference. A deal-breaking difference.'

'He's never made me feel breathless and dizzy, as if he'd swept me off my feet.'

Not surprising: Howard was cautious and sensible. Which wasn't a bad thing, Bella thought, but the oc-casional bit of spontaneity wouldn't have hurt. And it might have made her sister's world complete—which clearly hadn't happened. On paper, Grace and Howard were the perfect match—both sensible and cautious—but there was a little thing called chemistry. Without that, life would be miserable. 'You can't spend the rest of your life with someone who doesn't make your world light up.'

Grace bit her lip. 'I think you're about the only per-son who'd understand that. Mum's going to be so disap-pointed in me.'

'No, she's not, and neither is Dad—they both want you to be happy, and if marrying Howard wouldn't make you happy then you definitely shouldn't marry him,' Bella said firmly.

'I'm not sure if he was in love with me, either,' Grace said.

'Of course he was—you're gorgeous and you're clever and you're nice. What's not to love?' Bella demanded, cross on her sister's behalf.

'I think we both loved each other,' Grace said softly, 'but not *enough*. I mean, we've been engaged for ever—who stays engaged for four years in this day and age?'

'A couple who's saving up the deposit for a house?' Bella suggested.

'Apart from the fact that we already have enough money for that between us, you know what I mean—if we'd really wanted to be together, we'd have got married years ago rather than waiting. We don't even live together,' Grace pointed out.

'Mainly because Cynthia of the Eagle Eyes and Concrete Hair wouldn't let her little boy shack up with someone,' Bella said. 'Is that why you got drunk tonight?'

'No. That was the cartoon you drew for me,' Grace said. 'Fifty Shades of Beige.'

Bella winced. 'Sorry. I meant it as a joke, to make you laugh and relax a bit. I knew you weren't looking forward to the golden wedding party.'

'But it was so accurate, Bel,' Grace said. 'I was the only woman there not dressed in beige.'

Bella couldn't help laughing. 'Ouch. I didn't think it'd be quite that bad.'

'Oh, it was,' Grace said feelingly. 'I really didn't belong there. I drank three glasses of champagne straight down to give me courage and I didn't even feel them, Bel.'

Which was really un-Grace-like. She always stopped

after one glass. Sensible, reliable Grace who looked after everyone else and was usually the one mopping up, not the one throwing up.

'I was just numb. And that's when I realised,' Grace said, 'that I was walking into a life I didn't actually want. In fifty years' time, I don't want to be sensible Grace Sutton, whose heart has never once skipped a beat, and whose mother-in-law directed the whole of her marriage.'

'If anyone could live until well past the age of a hundred, marbles intact and with an iron fist, it'd be Mrs Concrete Hair,' Bella said feelingly. 'You've done the right thing, Gracie. It's much better to call a halt now than to wait until after you married Howard and then have all the mess of a divorce to go through.'

'Really?' Grace didn't look convinced. She looked guilty and miserable and worried.

'Really,' Bella said firmly, 'and Mum and Dad will back you, too.'

'I just feel that I've let everyone down—all the work that's gone into arranging the wedding.' Grace swallowed. 'Not to mention the money.'

'But you haven't let anyone down,' Bella said. 'Well, except you should have told me all this a *lot* sooner, because I'm your sister and of course I'm going to support you. I hate to think that you've been miserable all these months when I could've listened to you and made you feel better. You're doing the right thing, Gracie. And cancelling the wedding won't be that hard.' This was slightly surreal; it felt almost as if she and Grace had swapped places and it was her turn to be the sensible, super-organised one instead of the one who needed rescuing. 'Just give me a list of the names and contact details of the people you've invited and your suppliers, and I'll ring them all and explain the wedding's off.'

'I can't make you do that!' Grace protested.

'You're not making me do it. I'm offering. That's what sisters are for.' She took a deep breath. 'Have you told Howard?' Was that why her no-longer-future brother-in-law had been so conspicuously absent?

'No. I'm going to do that tomorrow.'

A nasty thought struck Bella. 'Does he actually know you've left the party?'

Grace nodded and winced. 'I told him I had a migraine and was going home.'

'And he didn't even offer to take you home? That's atrocious!'

'How could he leave? It's his parents' golden wedding anniversary party.'

'OK, so he probably had to stay there with the Gruesome Twosome,' Bella allowed, 'but he still should've made sure you were all right first and at least arranged a taxi to take you home.'

'I'm sure he would've done, but I told him you were coming to collect me,' Grace explained.

'Hmm,' Bella said, though she wasn't mollified. What on earth was wrong with the man? Howard had been Grace's fiancé for four years and he hadn't even made sure that she got home safely when she'd told him she felt ill—whereas Hugh Moncrieff, a man Bella had met only a few minutes ago, had not only come to the rescue, he'd offered to help them indoors. So her new boss had a good heart as well as a gorgeous face.

Not that she should be thinking about that right now. Or ever, for that matter. Even if she wasn't officially off men, her boss was completely off limits. She needed this job, to get her finances back on an even keel. 'So what are you going to tell Howard tomorrow?' she asked.

'The truth—that I can't marry him.' Grace closed her eyes for a moment. 'And that means I'll lose my job and my home, too, Bel. No way can I go back to work at Sutton's, not when I've just split up with the boss's son—and in the circumstances I can hardly ask them to give me a reference to work anywhere else. Plus I've already given my landlord notice on my flat. I know he's already found my replacement and signed a contract, so I can't ask him just to ignore my notice and renew my lease.' She blew out a breath. 'I've really burned my bridges, Bel—and who knows how long it'll take me to find another flat?'

'You don't have to. Come and stay with me,' Bella said immediately.

Grace hugged her. 'I love you, sweetheart, and thank you for the offer, but your flat's barely big enough for one person. You don't have room for me to stay. I'll ask round my friends—one of them will put me up until I can find somewhere—and I'll sign on with a temp agency. If I explain the situation, I'm sure they'll understand about the problem with references and help me to find a way round it.'

This sounded more like her level-headed older sister, Bella thought. Planning. Being sensible. The oats were clearly soaking up what remained of the champagne. 'It'll all work out, Gracie. You know what Mum always says: when one door closes, another opens.'

'I know,' Grace said.

'I was going to take you out for sushi and champagne tomorrow, to celebrate my job—because I wouldn't have got it without you—but we can take a rain check on that, because I'm guessing you won't want to see champagne again for months.'

'Definitely not.' Grace winced. 'And you might've lost the job, because of me.'

'Of course I haven't. I'll talk my boss round,' Bella said, sounding slightly more confident than she actually felt. 'Go and have a shower, clean your teeth, get in your PJs, and then we're going to snuggle under a throw on your sofa and watch a re-run of *Friends*.'

'I love you, Bel,' Grace said. 'You're the best sister I could ever ask for.'

Even though they were total opposites, Bella thought. And, weirdly, tonight, it felt more as if she was Grace and Grace was her.

'You came straight to rescue me without asking any questions,' Grace said.

'Of course I did! You've done it often enough for me,' Bella said. 'And you're the best sister I could ever ask for, too, and I love you to bits—even when I don't understand you. Now go and get yourself sorted out. I'm going to raid your fridge because I'm starving, and I'm sleeping on your sofa tonight. Tomorrow, you can talk to Howard and we'll make that list and work through it together. And then things will start to look better. You'll see.' She hugged her sister. 'Nothing fazes a Faraday girl, right?'

'Right,' Grace said. 'Nothing fazes a Faraday girl.'

CHAPTER TWO

ON MONDAY MORNING, Bella left her flat at what felt like the crack of dawn. For the last couple of years, she'd been able to set her own working hours—meaning that she could sleep in until ten a.m. and work until late, which suited her body clock better—but she knew that she needed to make a good impression on her first day at Insurgo. Particularly given what had happened at her first meeting with the boss. She couldn't afford to put a single foot wrong from now on, not if she wanted to keep her job and get her finances back on track.

And getting up early would take her mind off what had been a truly lousy weekend. Seeing Grace—the person she'd always looked up to as a tower of strength, someone who knew exactly what to do to sort out any given situation—fall apart had shocked Bella deeply. Right now Grace was in the almost same position that Bella had been in six months ago: recovering from a wrecked relationship, worrying about her job and her home and her finances, and feeling as if the sun would never rise again.

OK, so Grace had been the dumper rather than the dumpee, in this case, and she hadn't lost her best friend and the contents of her bank account as well as her partner; but it was still going to be a huge change in Grace's life. Even though it had definitely been the right decision.

Privately, Bella thought her sister had had a lucky escape. Howard was a nice enough guy, but he was completely under his mother's thumb. Marrying him would've basically meant having the rest of her life run by Cynthia of the Eagle Eyes and Concrete Hair, the most cold and judgemental woman that Bella had ever met. And finding another job might just mean that Grace's new employer would appreciate her and give her the promotion she deserved. At Sutton's, Grace had been totally taken for granted. They'd expected her to work way more than her fair share of hours, under the guise of being 'almost family', but they hadn't actually given her any of the privileges of being 'almost family'.

Howard had barely raised a single argument when Grace had gone to see him on the Saturday morning and called off the wedding. So he clearly hadn't loved Grace enough to fight for her. And Bella thought her sister deserved a lot better than a man who was nice enough but didn't have a backbone and would never stand up for her.

Today was a new chapter in both their lives. And hopefully this one would be better for both of them.

Bella paused outside the Insurgo Records building. The basement was a recording studio and practice rooms that local bands could book as well as being used by the Insurgo artists; the ground floor and mezzanine comprised a seriously upmarket café—the sort that offered coffee made in a way that looked more as if it was some kind of laboratory experiment than a hot drink, but apparently brought out the floral notes in the coffee; and the top two floors were the record label's actual offices.

'All righty. Welcome to your new life,' she told herself, and went inside.

She was the first member of staff to arrive in the office after Tarquin, Hugh's second-in-command—to her relief, Hugh didn't seem to be there yet—and Tarquin handed her a design brief, a portable CD player and a pair of headphones. 'Welcome to Insurgo, Bella,' he said with a smile. 'We're doing a limited edition of coloured vinyl for Lacey's third single. She's one of our singer-songwriters. I've given you a rundown here of our target market, her career history, and the PR schedule. What I need you to do is have a listen to the album—the song we're releasing is the fourth track on the CD—and come up with some ideas for the vinyl cover and a promo T-shirt, based on what you hear. Or if you have ideas for other promo items, bring them along. If you'd like to have a second listen in one of the studios rather than working on headphones, just yell and I'll sort it out. And then maybe we can talk about it, later this afternoon?'

'That sounds fine,' Bella said, smiling back. She was being thrown in at the deep end, but she'd always thrived on that. And this was her chance to shine and prove they'd made the right decision in hiring her.

'This is your desk, over here,' he said, and ushered her over to a desk by the window with a drawing board and a computer. 'As soon as Shelley—our admin guru—comes in, we'll get you set up with a password and username. The meeting room's on the floor above, along with Hugh's office, the staff kitchen and the toilets. I'm over there in the corner, and I'll get everyone else to come over and introduce themselves as they come in.'

'That's great,' Bella said, trying to damp down the sudden flood of nervousness. She was good with people.

She knew she'd find her place in the pack and quickly work out how to get the best from the people she worked with. She always did. But these first few hours in a new role were always crucial.

'Is there anything else you need before you start?' he asked.

Yes, but she couldn't exactly explain why she needed to see the boss without making things awkward. But she'd just thought of the perfect excuse to go up to the next floor. Hopefully Hugh wasn't in yet, so she could leave the neatly wrapped parcel in her bag on his desk. Or, if he was at his desk, hopefully he'd be alone and she could snatch two minutes to apologise to him in person while the kettle boiled. She smiled. 'How about I make us both a coffee?'

'Excellent idea. Thank you.' Tarquin smiled back. 'Mine's black, no sugar. I'm afraid it's pretty basic stuff in the staff kitchen—tea, instant coffee and hot chocolate—but help yourself to whatever you want. If you'd rather have something fancier, you do get a staff discount downstairs at the café.'

'That's good to know. And instant does me just fine. At this time of the morning, any coffee works,' Bella said with a smile.

To her relief, she discovered that Hugh's office was empty. So she wouldn't have to confront him quite yet, then. There was a pile of post set neatly in the middle of his immaculate desk; she left the package and accompanying card on top of it. Then she boiled the kettle and made herself and Tarquin a mug of coffee before heading downstairs to her desk and making a start on the design briefs. And please, please, let Hugh Moncrieff accept her apology.

* * *

Hugh wasn't in the best of moods when he drove his car into the tiny car park behind the record label offices. His shoes had just about recovered from their ordeal on Friday night, and his dry cleaner had said that there would be no problem with his suit. But he hadn't been able to get Bella Faraday out of his head.

Worse still had been the slew of texts and emails and answering machine messages over the weekend from his mother, his brothers and their partners, all reminding him that his brother Nigel's engagement party was coming up and they couldn't wait to see him. Which meant that Hugh was in for another bout of familial nagging. Why was he still messing about with his record label? When was he going to treat it as the hobby it ought to be and get himself a proper job?

He knew what the subtext meant: he was the baby of the family, so they'd let him have his dream and do his degree in music instead of economics. Now he was thirty, they all thought it was about time he gave up his financially risky business and joined the long-established family stockbroking firm instead. Which was why Bella's comment about him looking like a stockbroker had really touched a raw nerve on Friday night.

He happened to like his life in London, thank you very much. He loved what he did at Insurgo—finding promising new talent and polishing their rough material just enough to make them commercially viable without taking away the creative spark that had caught his ear in the first place. Insurgo had made a name for itself as an independent label producing quality sound, from rock through to singer-songwriters, with a sprinkling of oddities who wouldn't fit anywhere else. Hugh was proud of what he did. He didn't want to give it up and be a stock-broker like his older brothers Julian, Nigel and Alistair.

But the question that drove him really crazy was when his family asked when he intended to find a nice girl and settle down. That wasn't going to happen any time soon. Jessie had cured him of that particular pipe dream. He knew his family meant well, but couldn't they see that they were still prodding a bruise?

His business, his heart and his music had all taken a battering. And finding a new, suitable girlfriend wasn't going to repair any of the damage. Sheer hard work and some quiet support from his best friends had rescued his business, but nowadays his heart was permanently off limits. And the music that had once flowed from his fingers and filled his head had gone for good. He didn't write songs any more. He just produced them—and he kept a professional distance from his artists.

He ran through a few excuses in his head. None of them worked. Even being in a full body cast wouldn't get him a free pass. He was just going to have to turn up, smile sweetly at everyone, and metaphorically stick his fingers in his ears and say 'la-la-la' every time his career or his love life was mentioned. Which he knew from ex-perience would be about every seven minutes, on average.

He collected a double espresso from the café on the ground floor—on a morning like this one, a mug of the instant stuff in the staff kitchen just wasn't going to cut it—and stomped up to his office, completely bypass-ing the team. What he needed right now was music. Loud enough to drown out the world and drown out his thoughts. A few minutes with headphones on, and he might be human enough again to face his team without biting their heads off even more than he normally would on a Monday morning.

And then he stopped dead.

On top of the post he'd been expecting to see, there was a neatly wrapped parcel and a thick cream envelope. It wasn't his birthday, and the parcel didn't look like a promo item. It was the wrong shape for a CD or vinyl, and in any case most unsigned artists pitching to him tended to email him with a link to a digital file on the internet.

Intrigued, he untied the ribbon and unwrapped the shiny paper from the parcel to discover a box of seriously good chocolates.

Whoever had sent them had excellent taste. But who were they from and why?

He opened the envelope. Inside was a hand-drawn card: a line-drawing of a mournful-looking rabbit with a speech bubble saying 'Sorry'. Despite his bad mood, he felt the corner of his mouth twitch. Whoever had sent this was saying they knew he wasn't a happy bunny—and Hugh had a very soft spot for terrible puns.

He opened the card to find out who'd sent it, and a wad of banknotes fell out.

What?

Why on earth would someone be giving him cash?

He scanned the inside swiftly. The writing was beautifully neat and regular, slightly angular and spiky—the sort you'd see on hand-drawn labels in an art gallery or upmarket bookshop.

Dear Mr Moncrieff
Thank you for rescuing us on Friday night and I'm
very sorry for the inconvenience we caused you.

*I hope the enclosed will cover the cost of valeting
the taxi, dry-cleaning your suit and replacing your
shoes. Please let me know if there's still a shortfall
and I will make it up.
Yours sincerely
Bella Faraday*

He blinked. She'd said something on Friday evening
about reimbursing him, but he really hadn't been expecting this. Since the parcel and the card had been hand-
delivered, that meant that their new graphic designer must
already be at her desk. Most of his team didn't show their
faces in the office until nearly ten, so she was super-early
on her first day.

And, although he appreciated the gesture, it really
wasn't necessary. His shoes had survived and the rest
of it hadn't cost that much. He really ought to return the
money.

He picked up his phone and dialled his second-in-
command's extension. 'Can you send Ms Faraday up?'

'Good morning to you, Tarquin, my friend,' Tarquin
said dryly. 'How are you? Did you have a nice weekend?
What's new with you?'

Hugh sighed. 'Don't give me a hard time, Tarq.'

'Get out of the wrong side of bed, did we? Tsk. Must
be Monday morning.'

Hugh knew he shouldn't take out his mood on his best
friend and business partner. Particularly as Tarquin dealt
with all the stuff Hugh didn't enjoy, and with extremely
good grace, so Hugh could concentrate on the overall
strategy of the label and actually producing the music.
'I'm sorry. All right. Good morning, Tarquin. How are
you? Did you have a nice weekend?'

'That's better. Good, and yes, thank you. I'll send her up. And be nice, sweet-cheeks—apart from the fact that it's her first day, not everyone's as vile as you are on Monday mornings.'

'Yeah, yeah,' Hugh said, but he was smiling as he put the phone down again.

Bella was leaning back in her chair, eyes closed, listening to the music. Lacey, the singer, had a really haunting voice, and the song was underpinned by an acoustic guitar and a cello. The whole thing was gorgeous, and it made Bella think of mountains, deep Scottish lochs, forests and fairies. Maybe she could design something with mist, and perhaps a pine forest, and...

She yelped as she felt the tap on her shoulder; reacting swiftly, she sat bolt upright, opened her eyes and pulled off the headphones.

Tarquin was standing next to her, his face full of remorse. 'Sorry, Bella. I didn't mean to give you a heart attack.'

Bella's heart was galloping away. 'You did give me a bit of a fright,' she said. 'I was listening to the CD—it's really good.'

'Yeah, we think so, too.' He smiled. 'Lacey's a bit of a character. She always performs barefoot.'

'Like a fairy.' The words were out before Bella could stop them. 'Sorry. Ignore me. Did you want something?'

'Yes. Hugh just called down. Can you go up to his office?'

Uh-oh. This must mean that Hugh had seen her parcel and her card. And she had absolutely no idea what his reaction was going to be. 'Um, sure,' she said.

'Don't look so worried. The boss knows it's your first

day, so he probably just wants to say hello and welcome you to Insurgo,' Tarquin said kindly.

Bella wasn't so sure. If that was the case, why hadn't Hugh come down to the open-plan office? She had a nasty feeling that she wasn't going to be hearing a welcome speech but a 'goodbye and never darken our doorstep again' speech. Clearly the parcel she'd left on her new boss's desk hadn't been anywhere near enough of an apology.

Her fears must have shown on her face because Tarquin said, 'His bark's worse than his bite. He just isn't a Monday morning person, that's all. Whatever he says, don't take it to heart, OK? Everyone else in the office will tell you the same—and if he does say something horrible to you, he'll come and apologise to you in the afternoon when he's human again. It's just how he is.'

'Right,' Bella said, forcing a smile she didn't feel. 'I'll, um, be back in a minute, then?' She switched off the music, scribbled the word 'mist' on a pad to remind herself what she'd been thinking about, and then headed for Hugh's office, her stomach churning. Hesitantly, she rapped on the closed door.

'Come in,' he said, sounding brusque.

Tarquin obviously hadn't been joking when he'd said that the boss wasn't a Monday morning person.

And then her jaw almost dropped when she walked in. The last time she'd seen Hugh Moncrieff, he'd been clean-shaven and wearing a formal suit. Today, he was wearing black jeans and a black T-shirt with the Insurgo Records logo on it, and his dark hair looked as if he'd dragged his fingers through it instead of combing it. Teamed with the shadow of stubble on his face, it made him look as if he'd just got out of bed. He should've looked scruffy and faintly disgusting. But the whole package made him seem younger and much more approachable—not to mention sexy as hell—and her mouth went dry. Oh, help. She really had to remember that he was the boss, not just another one of the team. That made him totally off limits. And, besides, she didn't want to risk her heart again. Which gave her a double reason not to act on the desire flickering through her—even if he was the most gorgeous man she'd ever met.

He indicated the box of chocolates sitting on his desk. 'Why?'

Hugh was clearly a man of few words when it came to work. Or maybe it was his Monday morning-itis. 'Why the gift? Or why chocolates?' she asked.

'Both.'

'The gift is to say thank you, because you went way beyond the call of duty on Friday night. They're chocolates, because I can hardly buy a man flowers,' she said. 'Did I give you enough money to cover everything, or do I still owe you?'

He handed her the envelope, which felt thick enough to contain most—if not all—of the money she'd enclosed with the card. 'My shoes survived, and the taxi and dry-cleaning bill weren't much,' he said.

She knew that wasn't true. The taxi firm would've charged him for valeting the cab and for lost earnings while the cab was out of action, being cleaned. 'I'd rather you kept it,' she said, putting the envelope back on his desk. 'To cover the inconvenience.'

'No need,' he said firmly. 'Is your sister OK? She looked terrible.'

Bella was grateful he hadn't mentioned the 'incident'. 'Grace barely even drinks, normally,' she said, not wanting him to think badly of her sister. 'Friday was totally out of character for her. She's the sensible and together one who sorts everything out; I'm the flaky and unreli—' She stopped mid-word, realising what she was about to blurt out. 'Not when it comes to my job, obviously. I'm very together where my work is concerned,' she added swiftly.

'But in your personal life you're flaky and unreliable?' he asked.

'Not unreliable, even—just the one who opens her mouth without thinking things through,' she said ruefully. 'As you've just heard.'

'But you rescued your sister when she needed your help,' he said softly. 'That definitely counts in your favour. Is she OK?'

'She will be,' Bella said. 'I've never known her to drink three glasses of champagne in a row, let alone on an empty stomach. I think that's why... Well. What happened, happened,' she finished, squirming slightly.

'Thank you for the chocolates. They're appreciated,' he said. 'And you have good taste.'

'I have good taste in a lot of things.' And then, when she saw the momentary flicker in those amazing blue eyes, she wished the words unsaid. 'I wasn't flirting with you,' she added quickly.

His expression said, *much*. 'Take the money,' he said. 'I don't need it. Use it to take your sister out to dinner or something.'

'Just no champagne, right?'

This time, he smiled. 'Right. Welcome to Insurgo, Ms Faraday.'

'Thank you, Mr Moncrieff.' Formality was good. It put distance between them. And it would stop her get-

ting crazy ideas about a man with a mouth that promised sin and eyes that promised pleasure. Ideas she most
definitely couldn't let herself act upon.

'Are you settling in all right?' he asked.

'Yes. Tarquin's given me my first brief and I'm working on it now. The limited edition single.' She paused.
'He said it was coloured vinyl. I have to admit, I don't
know that much about how records are physically made.
Can the vinyl be any colour you like?'

'Yes.'

'So you could do clear vinyl with little wisps of mist
running through it?'

He looked surprised. 'Yes. Would that tie in with your
design?'

'It's what the music makes me think of. Obviously it's
just an idea at this stage,' she said swiftly, not wanting
to put him off. 'I'll do some rough mock-ups of three or
four ideas, and then I'm discussing them with Tarquin
this afternoon.'

'Good. I look forward to seeing what you come up
with.'

She blinked, surprised. 'You're going to be in the
meeting as well?'

'Not that one,' he said. 'But when you and Tarquin
have agreed which one to work on, then you come and
convince me.'

'Challenge accepted.' The words were out before she
could stop them. Oh, for pity's sake. This wasn't about a
challenge. This was about...about...

Why had her brain suddenly turned to soup?

He smiled, then, and it felt as if the room had lit up.
Which was even more worrying. She didn't want to start
feeling like this about anyone, especially not her new boss.

'I think I'm going to enjoy working with you, Bella Faraday.'

There was a faint trace of huskiness in his voice that sent a thrill right through her. This was bad. She could actually imagine him saying other things to her in that gorgeous voice. Things that would turn her into a complete puddle of hormones.

No.

This was *work*. She was really going to have to keep reminding herself that her relationship with Hugh Moncrieff was strictly business. Maybe she'd ask her friend Nalini to put a temporary henna tattoo on her hand saying 'work'—written in Hindi script, so Bella would know exactly what it meant but anyone else would think it was just a pretty design. The last thing she needed was for anyone to guess how attracted she was to her new boss.

'Good,' she said. 'I'll get back to it, then.' She gave him what she hoped was a cool, capable smile, and forced herself to walk coolly and calmly out of his office. One foot in front of the other. One step at a time. She could run once that door was closed behind her.

She'd just reached the doorway when he said softly, 'Bella. I think you've forgotten something.'

Oh, help. She had to suppress the surge of lust. 'What's that?' Oh, great. And her voice *would* have to be squeaky. She took a deep breath and turned to face him.

He waved the envelope at her.

'Keep it.'

He coughed. 'As your boss, I'm pulling rank.'

If she was stubborn over this, she could lose her job. If she took the money back, she'd be in his debt.

Caught between a rock and a hard place. Or maybe

there was a way out. 'Then I'll donate it to charity,' she said. 'I'm sure you can suggest a suitable one.'

'Bella, this isn't a war,' he said softly, and she felt horrible.

'Sorry. It's just... I don't want to be in your debt. And I don't mean just you—I mean in *anyone's* debt,' she clarified.

'The dry-cleaning bill wasn't much, and the taxi firm is one I use a lot so they were pretty accommodating. And,' he added, 'I'm not exactly a church mouse.'

'Church mouse?' she asked, not following. Then she remembered the proverbial phrase. 'Oh. Of course.'

'Take the money,' he said softly, 'and it's all forgotten. As far as I'm concerned—and everyone else at Insurgo, for that matter—today's the first day we've met. And I'm notorious in the office for not being a Monday morning person. Nobody usually talks to me until lunchtime on Mondays because I'm so horrible.'

That made her feel better. 'Thank you,' she said, and took the envelope.

'Have a nice day,' he said, and that smile made her feel warm all over.

'You, too,' she said. But this time she lost her cool and fled before she could drop herself in it any more.

CHAPTER THREE

Even the idea was crazy.

Asking Bella was completely out of the question. She was practically a stranger; and she worked for him. Two huge reasons why Hugh knew that he should put this whole thing out of his mind.

Hugh paced up and down his living room. The problem was, now the idea was in his head, it had taken root. And he knew why. He could tell himself that asking Bella to play the role of his unsuitable new girlfriend was simply because she was vivacious enough to make it convincing. It was true enough. But he knew that the real reason was a little more complicated than that. Spending the weekend together in Oxford would give them a chance to get to know each other better. See where things took them.

Crazy. Stupid. Insane.

He knew better than to mix work and pleasure. Last time he'd done it, the whole thing had gone so badly wrong that he'd nearly lost Insurgo—letting down his business partner and the people who depended on them for their jobs. Only the fact that Roland, his other best friend, had bought into the business as a sleeping partner had saved him from having to shut the business down.

He'd worked stupid hours and he'd managed to stabilise everything, but he would never take that kind of risk again.

Strictly speaking, he knew this wasn't quite that kind of risk. Bella wasn't Jessie. She was part of the team, not one of his artists. She'd signed a contract with him rather than making a verbal agreement she could back out of because it would be her word against his. Getting to know Bella wasn't going to put Insurgo at risk.

But it still made him antsy. Since Jessie, he'd promised himself he wouldn't trust anyone with the battered remains of his heart. He'd keep an emotional distance. So why couldn't he get Bella Faraday out of his head? Why did he keep remembering that frisson of awareness when she'd kissed his cheek in the taxi? Why did her smile make him feel as if the room lit up?

And, more importantly, what was he going to do about it?

By Thursday morning, Bella felt as if she'd been working at Insurgo for ever. The rest of the team turned out to be total sweethearts, and they all shared a love of music, cinema and art. Everyone pitched in with ideas and suggestions, and nobody minded if theirs was passed over for a better one. And she absolutely loved working there.

The previous afternoon, they'd had a discussion in the office about which song fitted them, so that evening she'd made little name-cards for everyone's desk with a quick caricature of them and the title of 'their' song in place of their name.

It seemed mean to leave Hugh out just because he was upstairs rather than in the open-plan office with everyone else, so she made a card for him as well. 'I Don't Like Mondays' fitted him to a T, she thought.

That morning, as the rest of the team filtered in to the office and saw the name-cards on their desks, there was much hilarity.

Then Hugh walked into the office—clearly not in a good mood, again—and Bella rather wished she hadn't done a name-card for him after all.

'Ms Faraday—a word?' It was more of a command than a question, and his expression was completely impassive.

'Yes, Mr Moncrieff,' she said, and followed him meekly up to his office.

Even though he didn't say a word to her on the way up, she had a pretty good idea what this was about. He hadn't been amused at all by his name-card.

'I'm sorry,' she said as soon as he closed the door. 'We were messing about yesterday—' Then she stopped as she realised how incriminating her words were. 'Over lunch, that is,' she said swiftly, hoping that she'd saved the situation. She didn't want to get her new colleagues into trouble. 'We were talking about the song title that could be used instead of your name to describe you, and I drew the cards last night at home. It was just a bit of fun and I didn't mean anything by it.'

'You picked an appropriate one for me,' he said.

Though every single day seemed to be Monday, where his mood was concerned. He really wasn't a morning person. She winced. 'Sorry. Are you very cross with me?'

'No—and, just for the record, I don't mind a bit of messing about in the office. It helps creativity, and I know everyone on the team puts the hours in. As long as the job gets done on time and within budget, I don't actually care *how* it's done.'

'Then why did you want to see me?' Bella asked, now completely mystified. If he wasn't about to haul her over the coals for unprofessional behaviour, then what?

'Your hair.'

She frowned. 'What's wrong with it?'

'You were blonde, yesterday. Platinum blonde.'

'Ye-es.' She still didn't follow.

'And today your hair's red.'

A tiny bit brighter red than she'd intended, because she'd been so busy making the name-cards the previous evening that she'd left the dye in for a few minutes longer than she should've done, but she liked it. 'Yes.' Where was he going with this? 'Is there a problem with my hair colour?' she asked carefully.

'No, not at all.'

She really didn't understand. 'Then why did you call me into your office?'

'Do you have a boyfriend?'

Apart from the fact that you weren't supposed to answer a question with a question, what did that have to do with anything? She frowned. 'You're not supposed to ask me things like that. My relationship status has nothing to do with my job.'

'I know. I'm not asking you as your employer.'

She caught her breath. Did that mean he was asking her out?

No, of course not. That was totally ridiculous. Just because she had a secret crush on him, it didn't mean that her feelings were in any way returned. And in any case her boss was the last man she'd ever date. It would cause way too many problems, and she really couldn't afford to give up her new job. There was no guarantee that the receivers dealing with her former client would give her any of the money owing to her, because she'd be way down the pecking order in the list of creditors. And, with Kirk having cleaned out their joint bank account so she no longer had any savings to her name, she was stuck. 'Why do you want to know?' she asked, trying hard to sound polite rather than aggressive.

'Because I need you to do something for me, and I need to know whether I'm going to have to have a conversation with an overprotective boyfriend first.'

She was still none the wiser. 'Now you've really got me worried.'

He raked a hand through his hair. 'Bella, don't be difficult.'

That was rich, coming from him, she thought. Hugh Moncrieff was the walking definition of difficult. He was also the walking definition of sexy, but she had to keep a lid on that thought.

'Can you just answer the question?' he asked. 'Are you single or not?'

'I'm absolutely single,' she said crisply, 'and I intend to stay that way.' Just so it'd be totally clear that she wasn't trying to flirt with him—or anything else.

'Good.' He gave her a sweet, sweet smile. One that made a lot of warning bells ring in her head. 'Bella, remember when I helped you out last Friday night?'

The warning bells got louder. 'Ye-es.'

'Good.' He paused. 'I need a favour.'

So much for him saying that they'd forget what had happened. Clearly there were strings attached, after all. How *disappointing*. 'What sort of favour?' she asked carefully.

'I need you to be my date for a family event.'

That was the last thing she'd expected. Had she mis-heard? 'To be what?' she asked.

'My date for a family event,' he repeated.

That was what she thought he'd said. The words 'date' and 'Hugh Moncrieff' were a dangerous combination. 'Why?'

'A more pertinent question, in the circumstances, is "when?",' he said dryly.

OK. She'd play it his way. 'When?' she asked sweetly.

'Next weekend.'

What? 'As in tomorrow or as in next Friday?'

'As in a week on Saturday,' he clarified.

Talk about lack of notice. Did he think that she didn't have a social life? 'Where?'

'Oxfordshire.'

'Right.' She stared at him. 'So let me get this straight. You want me to go to a family do with you in Oxford-shire and pretend to be your girlfriend.'

'Yes.'

She folded her arms. 'Now I think "why" might be pertinent. And I think I deserve a proper answer.'

'If you want to know the truth, it's because you,' he said, 'will annoy my family.'

She looked at him through narrowed eyes. 'That's not very nice—to me or to them.' And it made her feel as if he was using her. Just like Kirk had. Even though Hugh was being upfront about it rather than pretending he loved her, the way Kirk had, it still stung.

'Given that you told me you were flaky and unreliable in your personal life, I think that's a fair assessment.'

He had a point. Just. 'It's still not very nice,' she said.

'I didn't expect you to go all Mary Poppins on me,' he drawled.

She resisted the urge to slap him or to say something rude. Just. 'That's because you don't know me very well. What do you want to achieve?'

He frowned. 'I don't know what you mean.'

'You said you want to annoy your family. What do you really want to happen?'

When he still looked blank, she sighed. 'Look, you're at point A and you clearly want to be at point B. What do you need to do to get from A to B, and is having a fake girlfriend really the most effective way to do it?'

He raised his eyebrows. 'That's a bit sensible.'

'Coming from me, you mean?' She rolled her eyes. 'It doesn't come from me, actually. It's the way my sister looks at things.'

'Your sister Grace? As in the woman who downed three glasses of champagne on an empty stomach…?' he said, with mischievous emphasis.

She put her hands on her hips and glared at him. 'Don't you dare be rude about my sister,' she warned. 'I already told you: that was really unlike her. It was due to special circumstances—and don't bother asking what they were, because I'm not going to tell you. It's none of your business.'

'Absolutely,' he said, disarming her. 'Actually, I like the way you stand up for your sister. And you have a point.'

'So why you do want to annoy your family?' she asked.

'This,' he said, 'is even more confidential than anything commercial I talk to you about.'

'That's *obvious*,' she said, rolling her eyes at him.

'You're my boss, so anything you say to me in this room stays in this room unless you say otherwise.'

'Thank you,' he said. 'Since you ask, the reason is because I'm sick and tired of them nagging me to settle down. So if I turn up to my brother's engagement party with someone who looks completely unsuitable, maybe they'll shut up and get off my case.'

She digested this slowly. He was saying she was unsuitable because of her hair? 'So basically you're asking me to play the kooky wild child. You want me to turn up with a mad hair colour, wearing ridiculous shoes and a skirt that's more like a belt?'

'What you wear is entirely up to you,' he said. Then he looked thoughtful. 'But, as you mentioned it first, yes, I think you probably have the chutzpah to carry off that kind of outfit.'

She still couldn't quite work out if he was insulting her or praising her. Instead, she asked the other thing that was puzzling her. Well, apart from the fact that he was single. Even though he tended to be grumpy in the mornings in the office, she knew he had a good heart. He'd rescued her and Grace when they'd needed help, even though at the time they'd been complete strangers— and at the time it hadn't felt as if there were any strings. Plus he had beautiful eyes and an even more beautiful mouth. The kind that made you want to find out what it felt like to be kissed by it.

She shook herself. That was something she shouldn't be thinking about. 'So why does your family want you to settle down?'

When he didn't answer, she pointed out, 'If you ask me to design something for you, then I need a brief to know what your target market is and what you want the design to achieve. I need to understand *why* before I can design something to suit. This is the same sort of thing. If I don't understand why you want me to play someone unsuitable, I'm not going to be able to deliver the goods, am I?'

'So you'll do it?'

'I didn't say that. I still reserve the right to say no.' If saying no was actually an option. Would her job depend on this? 'But if you tell me why and I agree with your reasoning, then I might consider it.' She spread her hands. 'Anything you tell me is confidential. But I would also like to point out that I do have a social life, actually, and I did have plans for the weekend.'

'I'm sorry.' He raked a hand through his hair, suddenly looking vulnerable. Which was almost enough to make her agree to help him, regardless of his motives.

Weird.

Hugh Moncrieff was old enough and tough enough to look after himself. You didn't get to be the successful owner of an independent record label if you were a pushover. He didn't need looking after by anyone. But that expression in his eyes had touched a chord with her. It reminded her of the look in Grace's eyes when she'd confessed that she didn't fit in with Howard's family and didn't think she ever could. That she'd felt trapped and miserable.

Was that how Hugh felt about his own family?

And why did she suddenly want to rescue him, when she was usually the one who had to be rescued?

'Of course you have a social life,' he said. 'And I don't expect you to say "how high" every time I ask you to jump.'

'Good,' she said. 'I'm glad that's clear.'

He gave her a wry smile. 'And I know I'm out of order, asking you to play a part.'

'It does make me feel a bit used,' she admitted.

'I don't mean it quite like that. I need help to deal with a tricky situation.'

'Just like I did—and you helped me, so it makes sense that I should return the favour.' Put like that, she thought, his request was much more reasonable.

'If it's possible for you to change your plans for the weekend and you do agree to help me by being my date, just be yourself. That'll do nicely.'

'Because I'm unsuitable?' she asked. Just when she'd started to feel OK about it, he'd made her feel bad again. Stupid. 'That's a bit insulting.'

'That isn't actually what I meant. You're confident,' he said. 'You're direct. You don't play games.'

'But you're asking me to play a game. Well, play a part,' she corrected herself. 'Which is pretty much the same thing.'

'I guess. I don't mean to insult you, Bella. I apologise.'

'Apology accepted.' She paused. 'So why do you need a date?'

He sighed. 'I'm the youngest of four boys. The other three are all stockbrokers in the firm started by my great-grandfather. My family would very much like me to toe the line and follow suit.'

She winced. 'Ouch. That's what I called you on Friday. I said you looked like a stockbroker.'

'I'm not one, and I never want to be one,' he said softly. 'Don't get me wrong. I'm not saying that it's a bad career—just that it's not right for me. My brothers love what they do, and that's fine. I'd support them to the hilt, but

I don't want to join them.' He gave her another of those wry smiles. 'That's why the label has its name.'

'Got you. Insurgo's Latin for "to rebel".' She wrinkled her nose. 'And, no, I didn't go to the sort of school that taught Latin. I looked it up on the internet. The only Latin I know is "*lorem ipsum*"—the stuff used as filler text in a design rough, and that's not really proper Latin.'

He smiled back. 'Actually, "*lorem ipsum*" is a mash-up of Cicero's *De finibus bonorum et malorum.*'

'Trust *you* to know that.' The words came out before she could stop them.

He laughed. 'I'm afraid I did go to the kind of school that taught Latin.' He dragged his hand through his hair. 'I love what I do, Bella. I like hearing artists play me raw songs—and then a different arrangement flowers in my head, and I can see exactly what they need to do to make it a hit without losing their original voice. I've never wanted to do anything else but produce music that I love—music that makes the world a better place. But my family worries about me, because the music business isn't exactly stable. Insurgo's doing well—well enough for some much bigger labels to have offered to buy me out, though I've always refused because I'm not going to sell out my artists like that—but I'm still at the mercy of the markets. We've managed to weather a few storms, but all it takes is one wrong decision that loses the business a lot of money, or for a couple of my biggest customers to go bankrupt and not pay me, and we could go under.'

'Tell me about it,' she said feelingly.

'I knew you'd get that bit. You've been there,' he said.

So either Tarquin had told him that she'd once had her own business, or he'd read her résumé. Or maybe both.

'Small businesses fail all the time,' she said, 'and I kept mine going for two years. If my best client hadn't gone bankrupt, owing me the equivalent of three months' salary, I'd still be a freelance designer now. But when one door closes another opens—and now I have a job I like here.'

'I take it back about being Mary Poppins,' he said. 'You're Pollyanna.'

'I'm just me,' she told him firmly, 'not a stereotype. But, yes, I believe in looking for the good in life.' She whistled the chorus from 'Always Look on the Bright Side of Life' and smiled.

'It's a good philosophy,' he said.

'You're right—you're perfectly capable of being a stockbroker, but it'd make you miserable. You're doing what you love,' she said. 'And there's nothing wrong with that. Why doesn't your family see that?'

He sighed. 'They have this little box ready for me. I'm supposed to fit in with a sensible job, a sensible wife, and two point four children or whatever it's meant to be nowadays. A *pied-à-terre* in London for me during the week, and an ancient pile in the countryside for the family, where the kids can grow up until we send them to boarding school.'

Was he describing what his own childhood had been like? 'I guess I'm lucky,' she said. 'All my parents and my sister want is for me to be happy and fulfilled.'

'Are you?' he asked.

She nodded. 'Are *you*?'

'Yes.' But she noticed that he didn't meet her eye. So did that mean he wasn't? And what, she wondered, was missing from his life?

Not that there was any point in asking. She was pretty

sure he'd stonewall her. Getting the information so far had been like pulling teeth.

'OK. So you want me to pretend to be your girlfriend, to show your family that you have no intention of meeting any of the criteria to fit that little box they've made for you. You already have a job they don't approve of, so what you need is an outrageous girlfriend to horrify them even more. That will be the icing on the cake, if you'll excuse me mixing my metaphors,' she said, hoping that she'd summed up the situation without missing anything.

'That's pretty much it.' He paused. 'So will you do it?'

'It's one way to get from A to B,' she said. 'But I think a much better one would be to sit down with your family and talk to them. Make them see how much you love Insurgo. Show them your passion for it. Play them the raw stuff, and then the final version with all the changes you suggested, so they can hear exactly what you do. Then they'll understand and be happy just to let you do it.'

'Maybe,' he said. 'But, even if they listened to me about my job, that's only half the problem dealt with. There's still the sensible wife they want me to have.'

She shrugged. 'You could always tell them you'd like a sensible husband.'

He grinned. 'You mean, ask Tarquin to pretend that he's my life partner as well as my business partner? I think Rupert—his other half—might have something to say about that.' Then his smile faded. 'I don't want a sensible wife. Or husband, for that matter.'

'What do you want?' she asked.

What did he want?

Never to have his heart broken again.

Which meant no more serious relationships. And it

had suited him just fine over the few months, dating casually and making sure that all his girlfriends knew that a diamond ring and a change of name were never going to be on offer. That he was looking for fun, not for for ever. And most of the time he didn't even bother with that. He concentrated on work. Though it wasn't quite the work of his heart any more. Not since he'd stopped writing music.

'What I want right now,' he said, 'is to get through Nigel's engagement party without being nagged about my choice of career or lifestyle.'

'You know that's not going to happen,' she said. 'That's the thing about families. They're interested in what you do, so of course they're going to ask questions and give their opinions, whether you ask for them or not. It's part and parcel of family life.'

Clearly she didn't mind about that as much as he did. Then again, she'd said that her family just wanted her to be happy. And she'd gone straight to her sister's rescue last week; he had a feeling that Grace would've come straight to Bella's rescue, too, if the positions had been reversed. His brothers certainly weren't batting his corner. They thought he ought to give in and join them in the family business.

She shrugged. 'So. Realistically, what's the best you can hope for?'

'That an outrageous girlfriend will distract them enough to stop them nagging me about when I'm going to settle down. Just for the weekend,' he added, wanting to make it clear that this wasn't a long-term thing.

'Weekend? I thought you said it was a party?'

'It's a weekend thing,' he explained.

She looked shocked. 'You're telling me that this engagement party is going to last for a whole *weekend*? Wow. I thought that my friends and I could party pretty hard, but we're all amateurs compared to that!'

'It's not that big a deal,' he said. 'We turn up for afternoon tea and cake on Saturday with the older relatives, and then we have a cocktail party in the evening. It's black tie, by the way.'

She looked thoughtful. 'So you want me to wear an unsuitable dress to the tea party bit, and something even more outrageous for the evening do rather than a proper little black dress.'

Oh, good. She understood and she wasn't going to give him a hard time about it. 'That would do very nicely.'

'And then what?'

'Um, we stay overnight—but you'll have your own room, don't worry. I'm not expecting you to share with me or anything,' he added swiftly. 'We'll have breakfast in the morning, go for a walk, stay for Sunday lunch because Ma will insist—except that'll be just my brothers and their partners and us, plus maybe an aunt and uncle or two—and *then* we can go home.'

'A whole weekend,' she repeated.

'The food will be excellent,' he said. 'And there will be pink champagne.' And then a nasty thought hit him. 'Unless last weekend put you off champagne?'

She rolled her eyes at him. 'That's mean. I already told you, my sister doesn't normally drink more than one glass. Last weekend was exceptional circumstances.'

'I apologise. Again.'

'Apology accepted, but I have a three strikes and you're out rule,' she warned. 'Do it again and I'll stand on your foot. In spike heels. I might be only five feet four, but I'm heavier than I look.'

'Got it.' The more time Hugh spent with Bella, the more he liked her. She made him feel different—she brought back the crazy, spontaneous part of him that he'd kept locked away since Jessie. Which was dangerous. Maybe he should call this whole thing off. For safety's sake.

'So what colour do you want my hair to be?' she said, cutting into his thoughts.

'Any colour you like. It's your hair.'

She smiled. 'Good answer. You're learning.'

'I'll pay for your frocks,' he said, 'and your shoes, and whatever else you want. Just tell me how much you need.'

'It's very tempting to say yes and drag you off to the fashion department in Selfridges with your credit card,' she said, 'but I guess it'd be more believable if I wore a charity shop find.' She paused. 'Or am I playing a gold-digger who expects you to bankroll her fashion habit?'

'I don't think you'd be a believable gold digger, because you're too independent,' he said. Again, so unlike Jessie, who'd always had an eye on the main chance. Except he'd been so in love with her that he hadn't seen it at the time. With Bella, what you saw was what you got—and that was refreshing. It tempted him to relax the rules where she was concerned. Part of him thought this was a bad idea; but part of him was intrigued enough to want to know where this could take them. 'A charity shop find would be good, but I meant it about paying for your clothes and what have you. Just get anything you need and I'll pick up the bill. You shouldn't be out of pocket when you're doing me a favour.'

'OK. I'll make sure I get receipts for everything. So I need outfits for a tea party, a cocktail party, breakfast, a walk and lunch.' She raised an eyebrow. 'I hope your car has room for a lot of luggage.'

'The brasher the better—and add that to your shopping list,' he said with a grin. 'And thank you. I think I'm actually going to enjoy this now.'

'Is it really going to be so bad, spending time with your family?' she asked.

And now she'd wrong-footed him again. He wrinkled his nose. 'I love them, but they don't see me for who I am. They don't listen to me. They want me to fit in their nice little box. That's the thing I find hardest to deal with.'

'So my job is to be their wake-up call. To make them see that by pushing you so hard, they're actually making you run just as hard in the other direction. Whereas, if they leave you be, you might just come up with a compromise that will keep you all happy.'

'I'm beginning to think that you should swap places with me and be head of strategy at Insurgo,' he said.

'Hardly.' She scoffed. 'I was working on design principles.'

'They work for strategy, too.' He paused. 'Thank you. I think I'm in your debt.'

'Strictly speaking,' she said, 'and, as you pointed out, I was in yours—you rescued Grace and me when we needed help. This is my chance to return the favour. And then we're quits—right?'

'Quits,' he agreed. 'That sounds good to me.' He reached over to shake her hand, then rather wished he hadn't when his palm started tingling. He really shouldn't start thinking about Bella in that way. He'd learned from Jessie that business and love didn't mix, and he didn't want to repeat his mistake. He was attracted to Bella— she was gorgeous and vibrant and she would make any man look more than twice—but he really shouldn't take this any further. They were going to keep this strictly professional. 'I'll let you get back to whatever you were working on,' he said. 'And thank you.'

'Last thing,' she said. 'What about an engagement present?'

'It's all taken care of. And the card.'

'How much do I owe—?' she began.

'It's all taken care of,' he repeated, cutting in. 'Really. I don't expect you to pay a penny towards this.'

'Can I at least take your mother some flowers, as we're staying at your parents' place?'

He frowned. 'That's very *suitable* behaviour, Bella.'

'Actually, it's common courtesy to take a present for your hostess,' she corrected. 'I don't mind people thinking I'm an airhead and unsuitable, but I *do* mind them thinking I'm rude and selfish. So. Flowers or chocolates?'

'She's a chocolate fiend. Dark. But you don't have to—'

'Yes, I do,' she cut in. 'Or the deal's off.'

And hadn't he asked her to help him partly because she was so outspoken and independent? 'OK,' he said.

'Good. And now I'm going back to what you pay me to do,' she said, and sashayed out of the room. As much as you could sashay in jeans and flat canvas shoes.

But the images in his head wouldn't shift all day. The curve of her backside. The confident, brisk way she moved. That spark of merriment in her blue, blue eyes. The curve of her mouth.

How would her mouth feel against his? Would she make his lips tingle as much as his skin? And how would it feel to lose himself inside her?

There suddenly wasn't enough air in the room. He

walked over to the window, opened it and shoved his head out. Maybe the noise from the traffic would clear his head.

It didn't.

'Get a grip, Moncrieff,' he warned himself.

This was strictly business. Letting his imagination loose was a seriously bad idea. He wasn't going to let himself think about what it would be like to touch Bella. To kiss her. To hold her close. This pretend girlfriend business was just to get him off the hook with his family. And, the more he kept telling himself that, the quicker he'd start to believe it.

CHAPTER FOUR

'ARE YOU SURE this is a good idea, Bel?' Grace asked.

'Going to Oxfordshire and pretending to be Hugh's unsuitable girlfriend? Possibly not,' Bella admitted. 'I did tell him I thought it'd be a better idea to be straight with his family and get them to see his passion for his work. But he's adamant that this is the best way to get them off his back—and I guess they're his family, so he should know the best way to handle them.'

'I don't mean just that,' Grace said gently. 'I mean getting involved in your boss's personal life.'

'I'm not getting involved in his personal life,' Bella insisted. 'Apart from the fact that I'm officially off men for good, I'm just doing this as a favour.'

Grace winced. 'To make up for me throwing up over him in the taxi?'

'No,' said Bella firmly. 'No.' Though he had hinted at it. Which had made it easier for Bella to say yes. Not that she wanted Grace to worry about it, so she kept that information to herself. 'He just needs someone to help him make his family back off. And I kind of fit the bill.'

'So you're going to a posh afternoon tea party wearing a skin-tight leopard-print dress,' Grace said.

'Yup. And I've got tiny, tiny shorts and high-heeled

mules for the country walk the next day. And, best of all, for the cocktail party... Meet my alternative to the little black dress.' Bella produced the curtains she'd found in one of the charity shops, flapped one with a flourish and draped it over one shoulder. 'Ta-da!'

Grace blinked. 'You're wearing a *curtain* to a cocktail party?'

'Not quite—it's going to be a proper dress. Only I'm making it from a curtain instead of from normal dress fabric. Em said she'd come round tomorrow, measure me, and we'll cut it out and run it up together.' Bella grinned. 'This is where going to art school comes into its own. I know loads of people who can help. I just thought, what could be gaudier and more unsuitable for a black tie cocktail party than a mini-dress made out of a curtain?'

Grace eyed the orange flowers. 'Um. Very nineteen-sixties.'

Bella's grin broadened. 'And it's so *The Sound of Music*, don't you think?' She draped the curtain over the back of her sofa, pulled Grace to her feet, and danced her sister around the tiny living room, all the while singing, 'How Do You Solve a Problem Like Maria?' but substituting her own name in the song.

'You're impossible,' Grace said, but she was laughing.

'I'm a genius. And I've just had another great idea. We can have takeaway pizza tonight and watch *The Sound of Music* together. I love that film so much. And we can sing "Do Re Mi" in harmony—I'll even let you pick your part.'

Grace hugged her. 'I know what you're doing, Bel. You're trying to distract me. But I'm OK. Really. The hard bit was last weekend and breaking up with Howard. The temp agency's found me some work, I've got a couple of weeks to find a new flat before I have to move out of mine, and you've been the best sister and most brilliant support anyone could ask for. My new life starts now, and it's going to be just fine.'

'I still worry about you,' Bella said. She didn't quite dare ask if this was how Grace felt about her, most of the time. Grace had had to rescue her often enough from some scrape or other.

'I'm fine,' Grace reassured her again. 'But, yes, we can order a pizza and watch a film tonight. That sounds good.' She took a deep breath. 'And if this engagement party goes horribly wrong next weekend, just ring me and I'll drive straight down to get you, OK? It's only an hour and a bit from London to Oxford.'

'It won't go wrong,' Bella said. 'I'm just playing a part. Even if I wasn't officially off men, Hugh Moncrieff is the most unsuitable man in the world for me. He's my boss, and dating him would make everything way too complicated.'

'So why,' Grace asked, 'are my big sister antennae suddenly twitching like mad?'

'Force of habit,' Bella said with a smile. 'But nothing's going to go wrong.'

The following weekend, Bella's confidence in that statement had evaporated.

Had she gone too far with her outfit?

What if Hugh's family had a blazing row with him over her unsuitability and it ruined the engagement party? That really wouldn't be fair on Hugh's brother and his fiancée.

Maybe she ought to pack some suitable clothes as well, in case she needed to change at the last minute. Or borrow Grace's car so she could make a quick getaway if she needed to, rather than letting Hugh drive her down to Oxfordshire. Or maybe she should just make sure her mobile phone was fully charged and she'd got the number of a reliable local taxi firm.

Plus she and Hugh hadn't set any real ground rules. What did playing his unsuitable girlfriend actually mean? Holding hands, draping herself over him—or even kissing him?

The idea of kissing Hugh sent her into a flat spin.

He was her boss. She shouldn't even flirt with him, let alone entertain ideas about kissing him. Even if he was the most attractive man she'd met in years. Kissing was totally off the agenda.

So why, why, why couldn't she get the idea out of her head?

Her stomach was in knots by the time her doorbell rang, just after lunch.

When she answered the door, Hugh was standing there, wearing one of his business suits. He looked utterly gorgeous—and Bella felt completely out of place in her outrageous get-up. Particularly when his eyes widened in apparent shock as he took in what she was wearing: a tight leopard-skin mini-dress with a wide shiny belt cinched round her waist and spindly high heels, a chunky bead necklace, and she'd styled her hair so her normally sleek bob was in wild curls.

'This is a bit too much, isn't it?' she asked, indicating her outfit.

'It's, um, *interesting*,' he said. 'Very eighties. Especially the hair.'

In other words, he hated it. She'd gone way over the top. There was cutesy retro, and there was a total mess.

She'd clearly crossed the admittedly narrow line between the two. She took a deep breath. 'Sorry. Give me ten minutes and I'll change.'

He caught her hand. 'No, Bella, you're perfect as you are.'

A shiver ran through her at the feel of his skin against hers. She had to remind herself sharply that she was doing this as a favour to him—acting the part of his unsuitable girlfriend—and that was all. Any attraction she felt towards him was totally inappropriate and needed to be squashed. Like yesterday.

'Are you sure this isn't too much?' she asked, doubt still crawling through her. 'Are you quite, *quite* sure it wouldn't be better to switch to Plan B?'

'Which is?'

'Go to the party on your own and tell your family how much you love Insurgo, that you're perfectly happy being single and that you don't need a romantic partner to feel that your life's complete.'

'I could, but they wouldn't listen, so it has to be Plan A,' he said softly. 'And I want you to know how much I appreciate this, Bella. I don't know anyone else who could've carried this off.'

'Really?'

'Really. I'm not flannelling you.'

She could hear the sincerity in his voice. He really thought that she could do this. And to have someone believing her on a personal level, someone other than her family… That made her feel better about herself than she had in a long time.

'I'm truly grateful,' he said. 'Now, where's your luggage?'

She picked up her large, bright pink suitcase and

faked a confidence she didn't quite feel. 'OK. I'm ready. Let's go.'

His car was gorgeous—sleek and low-slung, with leather seats that were amazingly comfortable—and she wasn't surprised to discover that he had a really good sound system, too. She was happy enough to listen to music until they were out of London and on the motorway, and then she turned to him.

'Can I ask you some questions?'

'Sure you can ask,' he said, sounding as if he reserved the right not to answer.

'We'll start with your family,' she said. 'Even an unsuitable airhead girlfriend would know who she was going to visit. I know you're the youngest of four boys, and we're going to your brother Nigel's engagement party somewhere in Oxfordshire. Everyone else in your family is a stockbroker. And that's *all* I know. Do you not think that I might need to know everyone's names, at the very least?'

'I guess,' he said. His voice was totally expressionless, so she had no idea what was going through his head. 'OK. My parents are Oliver and Elizabeth. Pa's recently retired and spends half of his day on the golf course. Ma's in the WI and does charity work. My brothers—Julian's the oldest, married to Poppy, and they have a baby girl, Sophia. Alistair's the next and he's married to Harriet. Nigel's about to get engaged to Victoria, and they're getting married at Christmas. I'm the youngest, and I'm taking my new girlfriend Bella Faraday to meet the folks. Anything else?'

'Yes. Ground rules. What does playing your girlfriend actually mean?' she asked. 'Holding your hand? Draping myself artfully over you?'

He blew out a breath. 'I hadn't thought that far ahead, to be honest. I suppose they'd expect us to hold hands. And for me to dance with you at the cocktail party. Which is a point. Can you dance?'

She couldn't help smiling because he'd set up her answer so beautifully. And, with any luck, it would make him laugh and relax a bit, too. 'Would that be with or without a pole, Mr Moncrieff?'

As she'd hoped, he laughed. 'Without.'

'I don't really tend to go clubbing,' she said. 'But I go to a dance aerobics class, so I can move in time to music.'

'That's good enough for me.'

But he hadn't answered her question fully. 'Anything else?' she asked.

He frowned. 'Such as?'

'Normally, people who are dating tend to, um, kiss each other,' she said. 'Especially when dancing and parties are involved.'

'Ah. Yes. Kissing.'

The car suddenly felt way too small. And was it her imagination, or had the temperature just shot up by ten degrees?

'Chaste kissing would be acceptable,' he said.

Right at that moment, she didn't feel very chaste. And she wished she hadn't brought up the subject, because she could just imagine what it would be like to kiss Hugh Moncrieff. To cup his face in her hands and brush her lips against his, teasing at first, and then letting him deepen the kiss. Matching him touch for touch, bite for bite, until they were both dizzy with desire and he carried her off to his bed...

'Bella?'

'What?' She'd been so lost in her fantasy that she

hadn't heard him say anything to her. She felt colour flood into her cheeks.

'I said, are you OK with that?'

No. It was way too risky.

But she'd agreed to play his unsuitable girlfriend. And she was the one who'd brought up the question of kissing in the first place.

'I guess,' she said, trying to sound cool and calm and completely unbothered. 'Next question.'

'Hit me with it,' he said dryly.

'Why are you single?'

He blew out a breath. 'You're very direct. Why are *you* single?'

Because she'd put her trust in the wrong people. 'I asked you first.'

He shrugged. 'I was seeing someone and it didn't work out.'

That was obviously the need-to-know version of the story, she thought. She didn't think Hugh was the type to be a selfish love rat—someone like that wouldn't have come to her and Grace's rescue when they'd needed help, the other week—so she assumed that he hadn't been the one to end the relationship. Had his ex broken his heart? But there was no point in asking him. She knew he'd stonewall her.

'You?' he asked.

'You summed it up for me, too. I was seeing someone and it didn't work out,' she said. She didn't want to tell him the whole messy story. More precisely, she didn't want him knowing that she was so naïve and had such poor judgement in relationships. Her best friend and her live-in boyfriend. Just how had she managed to keep her eyes so firmly closed to what was really going on between them?

'Was it recent?' he asked.

'Six months ago,' she said. 'And you?'

'A year.'

'And you haven't met anyone else since?' That surprised her. When he wasn't being grumpy in the office, Hugh was good company. And he was very easy on the eye. Surely he had women lining up for him in droves?

'I've been too busy concentrating on my business.' He paused. 'You?'

'The same.' Except it hadn't just been her romantic relationship that had crashed. Kirk had dumped her for the woman Bella had believed was her best friend since sixth form, taking that support away from her, too. And Kirk had quietly cleaned out their joint bank account, the morning he dumped her—which was why Bella hadn't had her normal safety cushion of the equivalent of three months' salary when her best client went bust, and why her finances were in such a mess now.

And there had been next to nothing she could do about it, because the money had been in their joint names. She'd talked to the bank, but they'd said that any signatory to a joint account had the right to withdraw however much money they liked, no matter how much they'd actually put in.

Bella would never make that mistake again. And she was really glad that she'd listened to Grace's advice and put her tax money to one side in a different account rather than keeping it with her 'salary', or she'd be in debt to the Inland Revenue as well.

'Let's just say I'm tired of always dating Mr Wrong and I'm happier being single,' she said.

'Works for me. Any more questions?'

He was definitely in his Monday morning office mode now. Grumpy and difficult. She decided that any other questions could wait. 'I guess we've covered the basics.'

'Good. If you don't mind, I'd better concentrate on my driving.'

Given that they were going to his family home, he probably knew the route blindfold, so Bella was pretty sure that this was just his way of avoiding any more questions. And she supposed he had a point. She knew enough to play her role. Asking him anything else would be intrusive, wouldn't it? She let him concentrate on his driving and fiddled quietly with her phone, until he turned off the main road and drove them through narrower country roads to the outskirts of a village.

'Here we are, then,' he said as he turned into a driveway. The fences on either side were in perfect repair, and huge lime trees lined the fences and cast dappled shade on the driveway.

Bella had known that Hugh was from a posh background, but she hadn't realised just how posh. At the end of the half-a-mile-long driveway was the most beautiful house she'd ever seen: an Elizabethan manor house built from mellow Cotswold stone, with floor-to-ceiling sash windows on the ground floor, mullioned windows on the top floor, wisteria climbing the walls which wasn't in bloom yet but would look stunning in a couple of weeks, and a wide front door with a spider-web fanlight above it.

'That's gorgeous,' she said. 'And I've got this weird sense of déjà vu—I know I've never been here before, but somehow I feel as if I have.'

'You've probably seen the house on TV,' he said. 'It's been used as a location for a few period dramas.'

Before she had the chance to ask which ones, he parked on the gravelled area outside the house.

'I see my brothers are already here,' he said.

There were two sports cars similar to Hugh's parked outside the house, along with a Range Rover, a Daimler and a Bentley. It felt almost as if she was walking into one of the period dramas he'd mentioned. And it was a million miles away from her own background. Was she really going to be able to pull this off?

'The grandparents and the aunts are here, too, by the looks of it,' he said. 'We might as well go in and say hello. There probably isn't enough time to give you a proper guided tour of the house before tea's served, but I promise I'll do it tomorrow. Ma's probably in the kitchen fussing about. She said afternoon tea would be in the dining room and the cocktail party tonight's in the ballroom.'

'Your parents have a ballroom?' She smiled to hide the panic that trickled through her. 'That's very Jane Austen.'

'It's probably been in one of the Austen adaptations. I can't really remember,' he said with a shrug. 'Which sounds terribly snooty, but it isn't meant to be.'

'Of course not.' Bella had the feeling that he was much more nervous about this than he looked, and somehow that made her feel a little less nervous. A little less alone.

'Imagine the kind of house parties they had back in Austen's time,' he said. 'I'd be off fishing or hunting with my brothers, or playing cards and drinking. But the women in the house party wouldn't be allowed to do much more than read or play the piano. They'd be under constant scrutiny, and there were all the intricate manners…' He shuddered. 'I hate that kind of stuff. I'm glad it's not like that now.'

'Isn't it?' she asked softly—because that bit about constant scrutiny and manners sounded personal.

'No.'

'It was for my sister.' The words were out before she
could stop them.

He looked at her. 'How?'

'I...' She sighed. 'OK. You're unlikely to meet her
again, but if you do and you tell her you know why she
drank all that champagne that night I might have to kill
you.'

'Noted. What happened?' he asked, sounding curious.

'She was at the golden wedding anniversary party for
her fiancé's parents. Let's just say that Cynthia of the
Concrete Hair—'

He blinked. 'Who?'

'Howard's mother. You know the sort of woman I
mean. Everything's all about appearances and she's so
polished that her hair is set like concrete.' Bella waved a
dismissive hand. 'And she watches you like a hawk and
judges you—usually unfairly.'

'Yes, I've come across people like that,' he said.

'So I think Gracie finally realised that if she went
ahead and married Howard, her life was going to be seriously miserable.' She grimaced. 'She tried to blot it out
by drinking champagne. It didn't work. So, for the first
time ever, I was the sister who did the rescuing—with a
lot of help from you.' She bit her lip. 'The wedding was
meant to be next weekend.'

'So Grace was a runaway bride?' He looked surprised.

'No. She didn't jilt Howard at the altar—she'd never
do anything that mean. But they'd been engaged for four
years and he never swept her off her feet, not *once*.'

'Being swept off your feet is overrated,' Hugh said. 'You're more likely to fall into a puddle of slurry.'

'Slurry?' she asked, not understanding.

He grinned. 'You're definitely a townie, then. Slurry is liquid manure. Used as fertiliser on fields.'

She pulled a face. 'That's vile.'

'Exactly how it smells. You always know when it's muck-spreading season.'

'It's not muck-spreading season now, is it?'

He laughed. 'No.'

'Good.' She took a deep breath. 'Righty. Time to play my part, I guess. Ditzy and unsuitable girlfriend with a terrible taste in clothes—that's me, right?'

'Right. And thank you for saving my bacon. I appreciate this. Even if it might not seem that way.'

He took their bags from the car and they went into the house. Bella noticed the sweeping staircase coming into the hallway and the Regency striped paper on the walls; the house really was gorgeous, and she itched to explore, though she knew it would be rude to ask.

Three dogs came rushing down the hallway to meet them, their tails a wagging blur.

'I forgot to warn you about the mutts,' he said. 'Sorry. Are you OK with dogs?'

'Very OK. I grew up with a dog,' she said, and bent down to make a fuss of the chocolate Labrador, Westie and Cocker Spaniel.

'This lot are Lennie the lab, Wilf the Westie and Sukie the spaniel,' he introduced them.

The dogs wriggled and shoved each other and tried to get closer to Bella. 'They're lovely,' she said, laughing. 'Hello, you ravening beasties. I'm sorry, I don't have any treats for you because I wasn't expecting to meet you, but

I can rub your ears and scratch your backs for you, and I'll play ball with you for a bit if you want.'

'Do that and they'll pester you for the whole weekend,' Hugh warned.

She smiled up at him. 'And that's a problem, how?'

A woman who looked so much like Hugh that she had to be his mother came into the hallway and hugged him. 'Darling, I'm so glad you could make it.'

OK, so now she had to be Miss Ditzy. Breathe, Bella reminded herself, and stay in character. She stood up and gave her best attempt at a goofy smile.

'Bella, this is my mother, Elizabeth Moncrieff,' Hugh said.

'Libby will do nicely,' Hugh's mother said. 'We don't stand on ceremony in this house.'

'Ma, this is my friend Bella Faraday,' Hugh continued.

'Like the scientist?'

Libby had perfect manners, Bella thought, and didn't even look the remotest bit fazed by Bella's outlandish dress. 'Yes, like the scientist,' she agreed, before remembering that she was supposed to be playing the part of someone who would probably never have heard of Michael Faraday, let alone known who he was.

'I'll just show Bella up to her room,' Hugh said hastily.

'She's in the Blue Room, next to yours. I hope that's all right?'

'Thank you, Mrs Mon—' Bella began.

'Libby,' Hugh's mother reminded her.

'Libby.' Bella opened her bag and took out the beautifully wrapped package of dark chocolates she'd bought earlier. 'And these are for you, to say thank you for having me.'

'How lovely.' Libby went pink. 'And I recognise that

packaging. These are my absolute favourites. That's very kind of you.'

'My pleasure. I'm glad you like them,' Bella said. 'Don't let Hugh anywhere near them. He's a chocolate fiend. But I guess, as his mum, you already know that.'

'Oh, I do,' Libby said feelingly.

'Let's go and put our things upstairs,' Hugh said.

'Come down when you're ready. Everyone will be in the dining room,' Libby said. 'And it's a pleasure to meet you, Bella.'

Bella followed Hugh up the sweeping staircase and all the way to the end of a corridor.

The Blue Room was enormous. It was very plain, with cream walls and a polished wooden floor with a navy rug in the centre, but what really caught Bella's attention was the ancient wooden four-poster bed. She'd always wanted to sleep in a bed like that. 'This is amazing,' she said.

'I'll put my things next door. I'll call for you in a few minutes,' he said.

Was Hugh's bedroom anything like this? she wondered. Were there things from his childhood that would give her a clue about what made him tick?

Not that she should be thinking about any of that. She was simply doing him a favour and playing a part. None of this was *real*, she reminded herself.

To distract herself, she went and looked out of the window. The room overlooked the garden at the back of the house: a perfectly striped lawn, with borders all full of tulips, and a stone wall at the end of the lawn with what looked like espaliered trees full of blossom. It was a million miles away from her own suburban upbringing. How wonderful it must have been to have a garden like that to run around in and explore as a child.

Then there was a knock at the door. 'Bella?'

'Come in.'

Hugh remained in the doorway. 'Ready?'

She nodded. 'I was just looking at the view. It's gorgeous.'

'Yes, it's pretty good. I guess I didn't really appreciate it when I was younger.' He took a deep breath. 'Let's go and face the hordes.'

She walked over to join him. 'Though you might have to roll your eyes at me to remind me to be Miss Ditzy. I already made a couple of mistakes with your mum.'

'It'll be fine,' he said. 'I know you're going to do a great job. That's why I asked you.'

'So you didn't ask me just because you were desperate?'

His eyes crinkled at the corners. 'That, too. But mainly because I think you'll do this brilliantly.'

Funny how the compliment warmed her all the way through. Maybe that was because he was being sincere.

Then again, she hadn't spotted Kirk's lies, had she? For all she knew, Hugh could be lying, too.

She took a deep breath. '"Once more unto the breach, dear friends."'

He laughed. 'It won't be that bad.'

Once they got downstairs, Bella wasn't so sure. The dining room held the biggest table she'd ever seen in her life. And every place was already filled, except two.

Hugh introduced her swiftly to everyone before they sat down. She'd already met his mother, but now there was his father, his brothers and their partners and baby Sophia, various aunts and uncles, and his grandparents. And it was all just a little bit overwhelming—especially as Bella could see the shock on all their faces, even though it was quickly masked and everyone was very polite to her.

She knew that she was playing a part and Hugh's intention had been to bring someone home who was so out of place that his family would stop pressuring him to settle down, but even so she didn't enjoy their scrupulous politeness. It looked as if this was going to be a very long weekend.

A maid came in carrying a tray with silver teapots and what Bella guessed were silver jugs of hot water to refresh the tea. Porcelain jugs of milk and dishes with slices of lemon were already on the table, along with a selection of finger sandwiches, tiny pastries, slices of cake and what looked like still-warm scones. A butler followed the maid, carrying a magnum of champagne; once everyone's glass was filled, Hugh's father made a brief speech and proposed a toast to Nigel and his new fiancée, Victoria.

The food was amazing, and in other circumstances Bella knew she would've really enjoyed it. It was a shame that she had to play a part. Until she'd had a chance to work out who was who and the best way to play it, she decided to keep quiet.

But then the old lady sitting next to her—Hugh's great-aunt Lavinia—went very pale and looked as if she was about to faint.

'Are you all right?' Bella asked her, worried.

'I do feel a bit odd,' Lavinia admitted.

'Can I get you a glass of water?'

Lavinia looked grateful. 'Yes, please.'

Miss Ditzy might not know what to do, but Bella couldn't possibly keep playing that part when the old lady clearly wasn't very well and needed help. Hugh wouldn't mind her breaking out of role for this, would he? So she had a quiet word with the maid to get some water, persuaded Lavinia to eat a sandwich, and sat quietly with the old lady until the colour had come back into her face.

'I think I might go and have a little lie-down,' Lavinia said.

'I'll see you up to your room,' Bella said. 'As long as you can direct me, that is. I'm afraid I don't know my way round the house.'

Lavinia patted her hand. 'Thank you, dear. That's very good of you.'

'My pleasure.' Bella helped the old lady back to her room, and stayed with her for a little while to make sure she was quite all right.

'You're a lovely girl, very kind,' Lavinia said. 'I can see what Hugh sees in you.'

Which was totally the opposite of what Bella was supposed to be doing. And she knew that Hugh didn't see anything in her anyway, apart from her being his graphic designer who was probably too outspoken and had been crazy enough to agree to help him in his even crazier scheme. She'd have to hope that her outrageous clothes would distract everyone else from seeing who she really was.

But going back to face everyone in the dining room felt really daunting. She didn't have a clue what to say. To her relief, Hugh met her in the hallway. 'Thanks for looking after my great-aunt. Is Lavinia OK?'

'She's fine—just having a little rest,' Bella said, and gave the same reassurances to Hugh's mother when Libby asked her the same question.

Libby gave her a searching look, then a nod of what looked very much like approval.

Oh, help. She'd really have to work at being unsuitable now. Hugh's mother wasn't supposed to approve of her. She was meant to stick out like a sore thumb.

After the tea party, everyone disappeared to get changed for the cocktail party.

'Come and knock on my door when you're ready,' Hugh said when they reached her bedroom door.

'OK.' Bella wished again that she'd brought a normal black dress with her, rather than going along with Hugh's plans, but it was too late now.

When she'd changed, she knocked on Hugh's door.

'Come in,' he called.

When she pushed the door open, she could see that he was sitting on the end of the bed, checking something on his phone. He looked up and burst out laughing. 'Well. I really didn't expect that. You actually found that in a charity shop?'

'The material, yes—it was originally a pair of curtains. One of my friends from art school specialised in textiles, so she ran this up for me.' She narrowed her eyes at him. 'Why didn't you expect it?'

'I guess I really ought to give you advance warning,' he said. 'The curtains in the ballroom are, um, exactly the same material as your dress.'

'The same material?' She stared at him in shock. 'No way. You're *kidding*.'

He coughed. 'Afraid not.'

She covered her face with her hands. 'Oh, no. I thought I was being so clever, having a Maria moment. It never occurred to me your parents might have curtains like this. I should've run this past you before we came. And I haven't got a spare dress with me.' She blew out a breath. 'Oh, well. I'll just have to change into the leopard-skin thing again.'

He came over to her and rested his hand on her shoulder. Again, her skin tingled where he touched her. 'Relax. Stay as you are. It'll be fine,' he soothed.

She rolled her eyes at him. 'I can hardly go to a party wearing a dress made out of the same curtains that are in the room, can I?'

'Actually, you can,' he said. 'You're the one person I know who can pull this off.'

She really wasn't convinced. And it didn't help that Hugh was wearing a dinner jacket with grosgrain silk lapels that matched the fabric on the buttons, a white pleated-front shirt, and a properly tied black grosgrain silk bow tie. He looked sleek, elegant and perfect.

She blew out a breath. 'You look very nice. Very James Bond, though I think you might actually have the edge on Daniel Craig.'

'Thank you.' He inclined his head in acknowledgement of the compliment. 'You look very nice, too.'

'In a dress that matches your parents' curtains and clashes with my hair?' she asked, raising her eyebrows. 'Hardly.'

'Remember, you have chutzpah,' he said.

'Maybe I should stay here. You could say I drank too much champagne earlier and have a headache.'

He shook his head. 'Have the courage of your convictions, Bella.'

She scoffed. '*Your* convictions, you mean. If we'd done it my way, I wouldn't be here and you would've shown your family how great you are at your job.'

'Let's agree to disagree on that one, because I know you can do this,' he said. 'Ready?'

No. But she had no other choice. 'Sure,' she said. 'Let's go.'

CHAPTER FIVE

BELLA'S FACE WAS pale beneath her make-up, but she lifted her chin high and pulled her shoulders back.

For a moment, Hugh thought about calling this whole thing off—someone in the house was bound to have a spare dress that she could borrow for the evening—but they'd agreed that the idea was to present Bella as Miss Totally Unsuitable. To the point where his family would all breathe a collective sigh of relief when he announced next week that the relationship was over, and they'd stop nagging him about settling down.

Bella was the only woman he knew who could pull off an outfit like this one. And he knew he was asking a huge amount from her. When they were back in London, he'd do something nice for her to make up for what he was putting her through right now. Maybe he could send her on a spa weekend with her sister or something.

He suppressed the thought that he'd like to take her away and make a fuss of her himself. She'd made it clear that she was single and wanted to stay that way. The same was true for him. Bella Faraday might make his pulse beat that little bit faster: but she was his employee, and that made her completely off limits.

They went downstairs and he ushered her into the ballroom. As they walked through the doorway, he felt her hand tighten on his arm just a fraction. And the gasps of surprise as people saw her and took in what she was wearing were actually audible.

The ground obviously wasn't going to open up and swallow her, and turning back time wasn't physically possible either. Bella glanced at Hugh for a cue about how to react and what to do—after all, this was his family and he knew them way better than she did—but he seemed to have frozen.

Nothing fazes a Faraday girl. The mantra she shared with Grace echoed through her head. Wrong. This had definitely fazed her.

Then again, Hugh had asked her to play the part of his unsuitable girlfriend. Which was exactly how she felt right now—awkward and out of place, absolutely not fitting in. What would an unsuitable girl do when she was the centre of attention? The only thing Bella could think of was to draw even more attention to her gaffe and ham it up a little.

She walked over to the curtains and did a little curtsey. 'I promise I didn't make my dress from these,' she said, gesturing to the curtains. 'Because my name isn't Maria and I'm fairly sure you're the Moncrieffs and not the von Trapp family—right?'

There was still an uneasy silence.

Had she gone too far? Or did she need to go further still? 'Well, then,' Bella said, and began to sing 'Do Re Mi' very softly.

Hugh looked at Bella, totally stunned. He'd had no idea that she could sing—especially this beautifully. It made him think of Jessie, and how his ex had bewitched him with her voice.

But Jessie wasn't half the woman that Bella Faraday was. Jessie was an ambitious, lying cheat, whereas he knew that Bella was completely open and honest. Even though at the moment she was playing a part: that was solely because he'd asked her to do it.

And right now all the heat was on her—Hugh's unsuitable new girlfriend in her even more unsuitable dress. He could hear Bella's voice faltering and he knew he ought to rescue her. Especially because this whole fiasco was his fault. He needed to step in and take the heat off her. Now.

She'd even given him the perfect cue.

Yet that would mean performing in public. Something he hadn't done since Jessie had walked out on him. And singing a duet... The whole idea of it made him feel sick to his stomach, bringing back the misery and disappointment he'd felt when he'd learned the truth about how much of a fool he'd been, and the dismay when he'd realised the ramifications for Insurgo. He really didn't want to do this.

Yet how could he be a snake and leave Bella to face everyone's disapproval alone? This whole thing had been his idea, and she was doing him a favour. It wasn't fair that she should bear the brunt of it.

It left him no real choice.

Taking a deep breath, he walked over to Bella and took her hand. 'Von Trapp, you said? I believe that's my cue.' And then he began to sing 'Edelweiss'.

Bella smiled, and to his surprise she joined him in the song.

It had been a long, long time since Hugh had sung a duet with someone. Jessie. Who'd sung like an angel, promised him paradise, and left him in hell. This should've made him want to run for the hills as fast as possible. Instead, it felt as if something in the region of his heart had just cracked a tiny bit, enough to let in some unexpected warmth. His hand tightened just that tiny bit more round hers; and when she squeezed his fingers back the crack around his heart grew just that little bit wider.

When the song finished, everyone clapped and the tension in the ballroom had dissolved.

Then Nigel came over to him. 'Hugh, I need a favour.'

Considering that he'd just almost wrecked his brother's engagement party, Hugh felt guilty enough to agree to whatever it was. 'Sure. What do you need?'

'Excuse us, Bella,' Nigel said, and led Hugh off to a quiet corner. 'The band I hired for tonight just called to say that their van's broken down and they're running an hour late. Would you play for us until they get here?' He inclined his head towards the baby grand piano in the corner of the ballroom.

'You could've had the pick of my artists. And they would've been here on time,' Hugh said mildly.

'I know, but the singer of the band happens to be Vicky's friend. Vicky asked her to do it before I had a chance to suggest asking you to recommend someone.'

Hugh laughed. 'Nice save.'

'I know I'm asking a lot of you,' Nigel said softly. 'I know why you don't play in public any more.'

Because of Jessie's betrayal. It had sucked all the joy out of music for him. He didn't write songs any more. Today was the first time he'd sung in public since she'd left. Right now though, he was punch-drunk, not quite sure how he felt—happy and sad were all mixed up together, with him smack in the centre of the whirlpool.

'Yeah.' Hugh took a deep breath. This was a big ask. But, in the circumstances, there wasn't a nice way to say no. And Hugh did love his brother. This was his chance to help, to do something nice for his family. How could he turn that down? 'All right. I'll play until the band gets here. But I'm not singing any more, and neither is Bella, OK?'

'OK.' Nigel patted his shoulder. 'Thanks. I appreciate it.'

Hugh walked back over to Bella. 'Will you be OK if I play the piano for Nigel and Victoria until the band turns up?' he asked.

'Sure,' she said, giving him what looked like a brave smile. Clearly she didn't think she'd be OK at all.

'Of course she will. I'll look after her,' his mother said, coming over and catching the end of the conversation.

That was almost what Hugh was most afraid of.

But before he could say anything his mother had swept Bella away and Nigel was looking anxiously towards the piano. What could he do but give in and sit down at the baby grand? 'Let's get your party started, O brother mine,' he said and began to play.

'I think you need some champagne after that, Bella,' Libby said, and snaffled a glass from the nearest waiter.

'I'm so sorry, Mrs Moncrieff,' Bella said, accepting the glass. 'About the dress. And… And…' She shook her head, not knowing where to start. Just that she needed to apologise. She'd thought she was being so clever, making a dress out of a curtain. And she'd ended up being horrifically rude. This wasn't who she was. At all. And it made her squirm inside. She'd come here under false pretences and she'd behaved appallingly.

'It's Libby,' Hugh's mother reminded her gently. 'My dear, I can see exactly why Hugh fell for you.' Libby patted her arm. 'What you did just now—that was very brave.'

'Or very foolish in the first place,' Bella said softly. There was a huge lump in her throat. She really hadn't expected Hugh to come to her rescue like that. The last time a man had left her in a sticky situation, he'd left her to deal with it alone. Yet Hugh had been right there by her side, supporting her and sorting it out with her. 'I didn't know Hugh could sing like that—or that he could play the piano.' Considering that Hugh owned a record label and he'd told her how much he loved producing the songs and turning them from raw material to the finished product, she should've guessed that music was more than just a money-making venture to him. But Hugh wasn't listed on Insurgo's website as one of the label's artists, and nobody in the office had even hinted that he'd ever been any kind of performer. He hadn't even sung along with the music in the car on the way to Oxfordshire.

But she'd overheard Nigel saying something about knowing why Hugh didn't play in public any more. Something really awful must've happened. And there was no way she could possibly ask Hugh about it, not without opening up what might be some very painful scars. She'd have to tread very carefully.

'Hugh was very cagey when I asked him about how you'd met,' Libby said. 'Are you one of his artists?'

Bella winced. 'Not *quite* in the way you think. I'm not a singer and I don't play an instrument.'

Was it her imagination, or did Libby Moncrieff suddenly look relieved? And why? Did that have something to do with the reason why Hugh didn't play in public?

'So how did you meet?' Libby asked.

Bella could hardly be completely honest about that, either. Not unless she wanted to tell a story that made her sister look bad, and that wasn't fair. The best she could do was give the bare bones of the truth. Which would probably be the safest thing in any case, because then she wouldn't have to remember which fibs she'd told and end up in a muddle. 'I'm an artist—and by that I mean a graphic designer, not a recording artist—and Tarquin interviewed me for the job at Insurgo.'

'Ah.'

That earlier look of relief hadn't been her imagination, then, because Libby suddenly looked wary again.

Was Insurgo the problem? Hugh had said that his family worried about him because the music business was so risky. Maybe this was her chance to bat his corner for him and get his mother to see just how good he was at his job and how much the recording label meant to him.

'As I said, I'm not a singer,' Bella said, 'but I do like music, and Insurgo produces some of the very best music around. I used to be a freelance designer, but my best client went bust a few months ago, owing me rather a lot of money. My parents would've bailed me out if I'd told them, but I wanted to stand on my own two feet rather than rely on them—so that's why I applied to Insurgo when I saw the job advertised. Hugh had nothing to do with me getting the job. Tarquin interviewed me.' She spread her hands. 'I didn't even meet Hugh until after I'd accepted the job.'

To her relief, Libby looked a bit less wary again.

She took a sip of champagne. 'It's a good place to work. I've never been anywhere with a sense of team spirit like there is at Insurgo. Everyone looks out for each other. And the musicians all love coming in to the office because they feel we listen to them. Hugh doesn't treat them just as cash cows or as if they're stupid. He listens to what they want, and he gives them advice—and they listen to him because they know he wants to help them be the best they can be. They know he'll take their raw material and polish it—but he'll still keep their vision.'

Libby nodded, but said nothing.

'Insurgo wouldn't be the success it is without Hugh. He's its heart,' Bella said. 'And he really loves what he does. There aren't many people who can say that nowadays.'

'But the music business is so precarious,' Libby said.

'It is,' Bella agreed. 'But Hugh doesn't take stupid risks. He's really sharp and he makes exactly the right business decisions—though nobody in the office will ever ask him anything on a Monday morning.'

'Why not?'

'He's, um, not really a Monday morning person. Though I guess, as his mum, you already know that.' She smiled, and told Libby about the name-cards she'd made for everyone in the office.

Libby laughed. 'You didn't do that on a Monday morning, I hope.'

Bella laughed back, feeling properly at ease for the first time since she'd arrived. 'I wouldn't have dared. No, it was a Thursday. And he was still pretty grumpy.'

'So you can sketch people really quickly?'

'Not just people.' Bella fished in her bag and took out a pen and a small spiral-bound notebook. 'Give me a few seconds,' she said with a smile. She sketched swiftly. Then she handed the notebook with the line drawing to Libby. Sitting patiently next to a cake and wearing hopeful expressions as they stared at it were Lennie, Wilf and Sukie.

'Oh, that's wonderful,' Libby said. 'May I keep it?'

'Of course.' Bella detached the page and handed it to her.

'Thank you. So what exactly did you draw on Hugh's name-card?' Libby asked, sounding intrigued.

'You're his mother. I can hardly show you.'

Libby laughed. 'I used to have to get him out of bed on Monday mornings when he was a teen. I think I've seen him at his very grumpiest.'

'Well, if you put it that way,' Bella said, 'how can I resist?' She drew another sketch. And, before she realised it, she had a circle of people around her, all wanting to see her drawings and all asking for a sketch.

Oh, help. She was supposed to be playing Miss Ditzy and Unsuitable, not making friends with everyone the way she always did. Hugh was going to be furious. She'd just have to work out how to extract herself from this before the band turned up and he could leave the piano.

Hugh finally managed to get away from the piano when the band turned up, all flustered and apologetic. He went to rescue Bella from his mother, only to find her right in the middle of a crowd. Everyone around her was laughing and joking, and he noticed that she had a pen and paper in her hand.

She looked as if she belonged.

Oh, no. That wasn't supposed to happen. His bright idea was going completely pear-shaped. His family had obviously seen way beyond Bella's surface unsuitability. And Bella herself had clearly forgotten that she was playing the part of Miss Ditzy and Unsuitable.

Then again, hadn't he also told her just to be herself? Which was exactly what she was doing. Bella, the graphic artist, the woman who'd fitted in to their team at the office as if she'd been there since day one.

Right now, she lit up the room. Which scared him and drew him in equal measures. He wanted her—but he didn't want to risk his whole life imploding again, the way it had after Jessie. He needed to be sensible about this. And right now the sensible thing to do would be to get her out of there before she said anything that made his family guess at the truth.

And she was meant to be his girlfriend, so everyone would expect him to walk over and drape his arm round her shoulders. 'Sorry to desert you like that, darling.'

She looked up at him, her beautiful blue eyes wide. 'Hugh!'

'But I'm here now. Shall we dance?'

'I...' She looked flustered. Which was pretty much how he felt, too, so close to her that he could smell her perfume and feel the warmth of her body against his.

'May I finish my sketch first?' she asked.

'Sure.' He took a step back. Putting a bit of distance between them was probably a good idea, given that right now he wanted to pull her closer.

Hugh had seen what she could produce at the Insurgo office, but he'd never actually watched her working before. And he was amazed by how deft her hands were. He also noticed how she caught the tip of her tongue between her teeth when she was concentrating, and it made him want to kiss her.

Maybe dancing with her would be a bad idea after all. It would make her way, way too tempting.

But then she finished a sketch of Lennie with his father—lightning fast and seriously good—and handed it over to Oliver with a smile.

'Thank you, my dear. That's marvellous.' Oliver kissed her cheek. 'And maybe I could ask you to sketch Libby with Sukie for me, later?'

'Of course,' Bella said, smiling back. 'But I'll require payment in advance, you know. You'll have to dance with me first.'

He positively beamed at her. 'With absolute pleasure, my dear.'

Amazing. Even wearing a dress made out of a curtain which matched the ones in the ballroom and which clashed badly with her bright red hair—two things that Hugh was sure should've annoyed Oliver Moncrieff immensely—Bella had still managed to charm his father. Just, Hugh thought, by being herself. She couldn't help it. Bella was the kind of woman who brought out the best in people.

He led her off to the other side of the dance floor. 'I was going to apologise for throwing you to the wolves, but it looks to me as if you've managed to turn them all into little fluffy-wuffy lapdogs.'

She laughed. 'Hugh, don't be so mean. Your family's nice.'

He scowled. 'Maybe. When they're not nagging me.'

'Really, Hugh. They're *nice*.' She blew out a breath. 'And I should be apologising to you. I'm afraid I kind of forgot to be unsuitable. I was telling your mum about the name-cards I did in the office last week, and I ended up drawing the dogs for her, and...' She bit her lip, and Hugh had to suppress the urge to kiss the sting away. 'It snowballed a little bit. Sorry. I'll remember to be dim and scatty and unsuitable for the rest of the weekend, I promise.'

'Hmm,' Hugh said. He didn't think she'd be able to remember it for very long. Because he realised now that Bella wasn't a natural deceiver. What you saw was what you got. There were no hidden agendas. 'It's as much my fault as it is yours. I shouldn't have left you on your own.'

'But you couldn't have refused to help your brother.' She paused and gave him a curious look. 'I didn't know you could play the piano.'

'Lavinia taught me.'

'Lavinia, as in your great-aunt I sat next to this afternoon?'

He nodded. 'Before arthritis wrecked her hands, she was an amazing pianist.'

She frowned. 'So your family does understand about music, then.'

'Lavinia does,' he admitted. 'The rest don't. They still think I should give it up and join the family business.'

She looked thoughtful. 'So you play and you sing— I've heard that for myself. I'm guessing that you probably write your own stuff, too.'

He had. Once upon a time. Not any more.

She wasn't letting it go. She ignored his silence. 'And you own a record company. Do you ever record anything of your own?'

'No,' he said, knowing that he sounded abrupt and rude, but not being able to help himself.

But it didn't seem to put Bella off. 'Why not?' she asked. 'You're good. And I'm not just saying that because you're my boss. You, a piano and a love song— you'd have women swooning all round the globe. You'd make gazillions for the label.'

Hugh had written songs for Jessie, and he'd thought about recording them as duets with her. Then Jessie had dropped her bombshell that she was moving to another record label instead of signing the new contract with Insurgo, and by the way she'd met someone else…who just so happened to be the head of her new label.

And then Hugh had realised that maybe Jessie had never loved him at all. She'd just seen him as a stepping stone in her career, and it looked as if she was doing exactly the same with her new man. He'd been so shocked and hurt that he hadn't written anything since, and he couldn't remember the last time he'd touched the piano; the joy he'd once found in playing felt tainted with memories of her betrayal. Tonight was the first time he'd sung with anyone since he'd broken up with Jessie. The first time he'd played in public again.

And he didn't want to analyse that too closely. Or why it had felt so natural to sing with Bella, after the initial shock.

'I don't want to be a performer,' he said. 'I prefer being a producer. Seeing the rough diamond of the songs and how I can make them shine. You know, like Lacey's album—putting the cello in and a double bass made it just that bit more haunting and gave the sound some depth.'

'Fair enough.' She shrugged. 'I think I understand where you're coming from, because for me it's the other way round. I absolutely love designing, but I wouldn't want to own or run a gallery. The idea of having to organise a bunch of creative people…' She groaned. 'It'd be like herding cats. No, thanks.'

He smiled. 'It's very satisfying when it goes right.'

'Each to their own,' she said.

Hugh danced with her all evening, only stepping to

one side when his three brothers and his father all demanded a dance with Bella. And then he found himself dancing with his sisters-in-law and his mother, all of whom were singing Bella's praises loudly.

'She's perfect for you,' Victoria said. 'Even if her dress sense is a little, um, unusual.'

There was nothing he could say to that. If he protested, everyone would take it as a token protest; if he agreed, they'd have a date set for the wedding within the hour.

'I really should rescue her from Pa,' he said, and fled in Bella's direction.

'Is everything all right?' Bella asked when Hugh was dancing with her again.

'I think our plan might have crashed and burned a bit,' he said ruefully.

She winced. 'Sorry. That's my fault.'

'No. You were right. It was a daft idea in the first place.'

'I'm glad you can admit when you're wrong,' she said with a smile. 'That's a good thing.'

'Mmm.' He wasn't convinced.

She stroked his face. 'Hugh. Let's just forget it for now and enjoy the party.'

Her touch made every nerve-end sit up and pay attention. He had to stop himself from turning his head and pressing a kiss into her palm. Distance. He needed a tiny bit of distance between them, before he lost his head completely and gave in to his body's urging. He snagged a couple of glasses from one of the waiters and toasted her. 'I still can't believe you stood up there in front of those curtains, in that dress, and sang "Do Re Mi".'

'Says Captain von Trapp,' she retorted with a grin.

'Oh, please.' He rolled his eyes. 'Ma loves *The Sound of Music*.'

'So do I. It's one of the best films ever.' She hummed a snatch of 'My Favourite Things'.

'I hated that film,' Hugh said.

She blinked at him, clearly taken aback. 'Why?'

'The way the guy just ignored his kids made me so angry. And it wasn't so much a stick the guy had up his backside as a whole tree.'

'And you don't?' she teased.

What? Hugh stared at her in surprise. Was she saying that she thought he was stuffy? 'No, I don't,' he said, faintly put out.

'Prove it,' she challenged.

He narrowed his eyes at her. 'How?'

'Dance the samba with me.' She raised her eyebrows at him. 'After all, this is a party, and the samba is the best party dance I know.'

'Sorry.' He spread his hands. 'I would, but I'm afraid I don't know the steps.' It was a feeble excuse, but a valid one. If the samba meant dancing close to her and touching her... That would be way too risky. He needed to be sensible about this, not getting closer to her.

'It's easy. I'll teach you. Gracie and I go to a dance aerobics class where half the moves are based on samba.' She grinned. 'Just follow my lead.' Then she paused, batted her eyelashes at him, and drawled, 'Unless you can't take direction from a woman?'

He had the distinct impression that she was flirting with him. Even though he knew he ought to resist, he found himself flirting right back. 'I can take direction.' He stared at her mouth. 'When it's *appropriate*.'

Her skin heated, then, clashing spectacularly with her hair. 'Hugh!'

And her voice was all breathy. He was about to tease her when he realised that he couldn't speak, either, because right now his head was full of the idea of kissing her. And that breathiness in her voice was incredibly sexy. His mouth was actually tingling. All he had to do was lean forward and touch his lips to hers…

They ought to stop this.

Right now.

As if she was channelling his thoughts, she muttered, 'Back in a moment.'

But what she did next was to go and speak to the band. He recognised the song from the first couple of bars: 'Livin' la Vida Loca'.

So Bella wasn't going to let him off. To pay him back for making her blush, she taught him how to samba, making him repeat the basic steps and arm actions until his movements were fluid. He was surprised by how much he enjoyed the bouncy, shimmery nature of the steps.

Other people were watching them, but when Bella realised that she was having none of it. As the band continued to play songs with a similar beat, she went round and taught everyone else in the room how to do the basic steps. The women seemed to cotton on much quicker than the men—which didn't surprise him that much, because hadn't Bella said something about learning this kind of thing at an aerobics class?—but finally the whole room was dancing. Including relatives Hugh had never actually seen get up on the dance floor before.

How on earth had she managed that?

'You certainly know how to get a party going,' he said when she came back over to him.

She laughed and tossed her hair back. 'I *love* parties.'

He could tell. She was really lit up from the inside, and it was infectious. Being with her made him smile and forget just about everything else. How long had it been since he'd last felt this happy and carefree?

Then the band slowed it all down again. He held out one hand to her. 'May I have this dance, Ms Faraday?'

She gave him a shy smile and took his hand. 'Of course, Mr Moncrieff.'

He drew her into his arms and held her close, swaying with her. Weird how she fitted perfectly into his arms, all warm and soft and sweet. Maybe the romance of the engagement party had got to him, or maybe he'd drunk too much champagne, but he couldn't resist holding her just that little bit closer, dancing cheek to cheek with her. He could smell the soft floral scent she wore—gardenia, perhaps? It was enchanting: much like Bella herself.

And from dancing cheek to cheek it was the tiniest, tiniest move to kissing her. All he had to do was twist his head ever so slightly and brush the corner of her mouth with his lips.

Should he?

And what would she do if he did?

If she moved away, he'd stop, he promised himself.

Except she didn't move away. When he kissed the corner of her mouth, she twisted her head ever so slightly towards him, so her mouth brushed against his properly.

And Hugh was completely lost.

He tightened his arms round her and kissed her again, teasing her mouth with tiny, nibbling kisses until she let her lips part and he could deepen the kiss. It felt as if he were floating on air. Every sense was filled by her. And it had been a long, long time since he'd felt anything even approaching this.

He wasn't sure how long it was until he broke the kiss. But her mouth was reddened and her eyes were wide and bemused; he was pretty sure he looked in a similar state.

They needed to get out of here, before someone noticed or commented.

'Come with me?' he asked softly. 'Away from the crowd?'

She nodded, and he tangled his fingers with hers and led her quietly out of the ballroom and down the corridor to a room he knew would still be in darkness.

'Where are we?' Bella asked when Hugh led her into a darkened room.

'The orangery,' he said.

Once her eyes grew accustomed to the light, she realised that one whole wall was made of glass, and the moonlight shone through onto an ancient chequered red and cream flagstone floor. All along the walls were massive terracotta pots containing what she presumed were citrus trees; there were a couple of what looked like wrought-iron benches between the pots.

'Wait,' he said, and let go of her hand.

A few moments later, she heard a soft click, and then suddenly the room was glowing softly with dozens of tiny fairy lights twined round the stems of the trees.

'Hugh, this is amazing,' she said in delight. 'It's magical.'

'Isn't it just?' he said. 'We had a film crew here when I was in my teens, and the set designer said this was where people would sneak off for some privacy at a Regency house party, among the lemons and limes and oranges.

She reckoned they'd have had candles and it would've been beautiful.'

'Just like this.'

He nodded. 'Someone suggested fairy lights as a modern take on it without the fire risk. Since then, we've often sat out here after the sun sets, just watching the stars, with the fairy lights on. And a heater, in winter, because otherwise it's absolutely freezing.' He came back to hold her hand, and drew her over to one of the benches. 'This is probably my favourite place in the house. Even in the daytime, it's lovely.'

He'd promised her a guided tour of the house tomorrow, and she intended to hold him to that. But right now, when he sat down on one of the wrought iron benches and drew her onto his lap, she couldn't think straight. All she could do was to put her arms round his neck for balance. And from there it was one tiny step to kissing him again.

Time seemed to stop. It was just them, the moonlight and the fairy lights. Nobody came out to find them or ask Hugh to play the piano or Bella to sketch. They could've been light years away from anywhere.

But they could still hear the music.

'Dance with me?' he asked.

Even though part of her knew that this wasn't sensible—it was too intimate, just the two of them in the orangery among the fairy lights—how could she resist?

They swayed together in the room.

Any moment now, she thought, he'd say something to remind her that they were both playing a part.

And yet he didn't. He just danced with her. Held her close. Cherished her.

It was so long since she'd been held like that. It made her feel warm inside. Warm all over. And when Hugh rested his cheek against hers, even though she'd promised herself she'd be sensible, she found herself moving that little bit closer to him. Turning her head so her mouth made contact with the corner of his. His arms tightened round her and he moved his head too, so his lips brushed against hers. Once, twice: and then he was kissing her with abandon, and she was kissing him right back.

She was dizzy with desire when he broke the kiss.

'Hugh—I, we...' She couldn't think straight. There was something important she had to say, but for the life of her she couldn't remember what it was. She just wanted him to kiss her again.

She trailed her fingertips across his cheek, liking the very faint scratch of stubble. 'You're beautiful,' she said. 'Poster-boy beautiful.'

He turned his head and pressed a kiss into her palm. 'Less of the boy, thank you.'

Oh, yes. He was all man. 'I didn't mean it that way,' she said. 'Just that you're beautiful.'

'So are you.' He kissed her again. 'You make me ache.'

She dragged in a breath. 'Ditto.' An ache of wanting, of need. He was driving her crazy with his nearness.

'I know this isn't supposed to be happening, but right now,' he said softly, 'I don't want to go back and join the others. I want to carry you up the stairs to your bed.'

The big, wide four-poster.

'I want to make love with you, Bella.'

A shiver of pure desire ran down her spine.

She knew they shouldn't be doing this. It wasn't what they'd agreed. She was his pretend girlfriend, not his real one. He was her boss. It could have major repercussions and she could end up in another financial mess. They really ought to stop this right now and remember who and where they were. She opened her mouth, intending to say that they shouldn't.

Then again, this wasn't real. And she knew neither of them was looking for for ever. Kirk had wiped out her trust in relationships, and from the little Hugh had said about his ex she was pretty sure that he felt the same way. He wasn't looking for The One, any more than she was.

They were both adults.

There was no reason why they shouldn't act on the attraction between them, just for one night.

So instead, she said softly, 'Tonight's just tonight. A one-off.'

His eyes looked almost navy blue in the soft light. 'No strings.'

'No promises.' She didn't believe in promises any more. 'No for ever.'

'No promises and no for ever,' he echoed.

'Then do it,' she said softly.

He kissed her once. Hard. And then he scooped her up into his arms, pausing only to switch off the fairy lights, and carried her down the corridor and up a quiet flight of stairs to her bedroom.

CHAPTER SIX

THE NEXT MORNING, Bella woke to find a warm body curled round hers. For a moment, she couldn't place where she was and why on earth a naked male body would be in her bed at all, let alone wrapped round her.

Then she remembered.

Hugh.

She went hot as she thought about the previous night. The way he'd kissed her in the orangery among the fairy lights until she'd been dizzy. The way he'd actually carried her up to her bed. The way he'd undressed her, and then made love to her until she'd seen stars.

Right now, the way he was holding her made her feel special. Even though she wasn't really Hugh's girlfriend, and they weren't in any kind of relationship other than that of employee and boss—just for a moment, Bella could imagine what it would be like if this was the real deal instead of an elaborate fiction. She'd spent the last six months feeling stupid and useless and pathetic, after Kirk's betrayal. Last night, Hugh had made her feel good again. Not just the sex, either. He'd danced with her, laughed with her—*believed* in her.

Would last night have changed everything between them? They'd agreed that this was a one-off. No strings.

No promises. No for ever. But could they still work together after this? Or would she have to resign?

They'd have to talk—*really* talk—and maybe redraw
the ground rules.

Nothing fazes a Faraday girl, she reminded herself.

Except the mantra felt hollow.

Right now, she really didn't know what to do. Did
she stay where she was and wait for him to wake up? Or
did she creep out of bed and get dressed—or would that
make facing him even more awkward?

Hugh woke to find himself curled round a warm female
body.

Bella.

He remembered the previous night in full Technicolor,
and panic slid down his spine. Why had he been so stupid?

It was a physical thing, that was all, he told himself.
It was obvious why it had happened. He hadn't satisfied
any physical urges for a while. Maybe it'd been the same
for her. They'd both drunk too much champagne, they'd
danced together, they found each other attractive, and
they'd just given in to the temptation.

He sighed inwardly. Just who was he trying to kid?

If he was honest with himself, he'd been attracted to
Bella since the first moment he'd met her. Her bright
blue eyes, her bubbly personality, the way she opened
her mouth and just said what was in her head without
thinking it through. Not to mention the way she'd been
there for her sister; Bella Faraday had a good heart. He
really liked that about her.

But he still shouldn't have let things go this far between them. They were going to have to talk, *really* talk,

and redraw the ground rules. Because Bella was a great designer, perfect for Insurgo, and Tarquin would have his guts for garters if she left the company just because Hugh hadn't been able to keep his hands—or anything else, for that matter—to himself.

He lay there, trying to think what to say. Even though they'd both agreed that last night was a one-off, would she feel differently this morning? And, if she did, how was he going to handle it?

He knew that Bella wasn't like Jessie. But he just didn't trust his own judgement any more. He didn't want to take the risk of getting involved with anyone, so it was easier not to start something that was likely to end up in a mess.

Eventually he became aware that Bella's breathing was no longer deep and even, and her body was slightly tense. Clearly she was awake.

Was she, too, remembering what had happened?

Did she, too, think about turning round and kissing him hello, the way he wanted to kiss her right now?

Or was she full of regrets and awkwardness and embarrassment?

Right now, he didn't have a clue. But he knew he was going to have to do the right thing rather than ignoring the rest of the world and making love with her all over again. They had to talk.

'Bella?' he whispered.

'Uh-huh.' She sounded worried.

He resisted the urge to kiss her bare shoulder. No matter how much he wanted to touch her, taste her, he had to keep himself in check. Carefully, he withdrew his arms from round her. Odd how cold it made him feel. 'I think we need to talk.'

'Uh-huh,' she said again, and turned to face him. 'OK. I'll say it first. I know we agreed that last night was a one-off, but it really shouldn't have happened at all.'

Relief coursed through him. If she knew it, too, then it meant that things weren't going to be awkward between them. They could still work together. He wouldn't have to find another designer.

He tried to ignore the fact that another emotion under-pinned the relief. It was ridiculous to feel disappointed, especially as he didn't want to risk starting another re-lationship. He knew he was better off on his own, con-centrating on his business.

'Last night was last night,' he said.

'Exactly. You know the Vegas principle?'

'The Vegas principle?' he asked, not quite following her train of thought.

'You know—what happens in Vegas, stays in Vegas,' she explained.

'Ah. Yes.'

'I think we should apply that to last night,' she said carefully.

He agreed. Completely. 'So you're not going to resign because I couldn't keep my hands to myself?' he asked.

'And you're not going to sack me because I didn't stick to our plan?'

Clearly she didn't want to leave her job, either. Which was a very, very good thing. 'Apart from the fact that I don't have any grounds to sack you, you're good at your job. Tarquin would kill me if I made you leave.'

Was it his imagination, or was there a flash of disap-pointment in her eyes?

He wasn't going to analyse that too closely. Much bet-ter to let each other off the hook instead than to get tied up with all the complications. And he definitely shouldn't tell her that he didn't want her to leave because he liked having her around. That'd be way too much pressure on both of them.

'What happened last night—we don't talk about it ever again. And it's not going to be repeated,' she said.

'Agreed,' he said.

She took a deep breath. 'So we stick to the plan from here on, and I'm back to playing Miss Ditzy this morning.'

'Uh-huh.' Even though he knew she wasn't very good at it. Yesterday, although she'd tried, her true self had just shone through the play-acting. And his family had responded in kind: warmth generating warmth.

If only he'd met her years ago. When he was still able to trust. But there was no point in wishing for something he couldn't have.

'What's the agenda for today?' she asked. 'You promised me a guided tour of the house.'

And he'd make very sure that the orangery wasn't part of that. Because then he'd remember how it had been last night and he'd want to kiss her again. It would be very stupid to put himself back in the path of temptation. 'Of course,' he said, 'and everyone's going for a walk between breakfast and lunch.'

'I have a really unsuitable outfit for that,' she said. 'Totally impractical spike-heeled mules that I can totter about in.'

'They sound perfect.' He paused. 'I guess we ought to, um, get up and face everyone downstairs for breakfast. I'll, um, go next door and have a shower.' Even though part of him would much prefer staying here and having a shower with her.

'Uh-huh.'

Was she relieved or disappointed that he was going? He hadn't a clue. And he wasn't going to ask. 'I'll knock for you when I'm ready, shall I?'

This time she definitely looked relieved. He winced inwardly. Did she really think that he'd leave her to find her own way through the house, and then face his family on her own? Or maybe that was the way her ex had treated her. Again, he couldn't really ask. Not without maybe ripping open some scars, and he didn't want to hurt her.

'See you in a bit, then,' she said. And then she closed her eyes.

Was she feeling shy? Or was she trying to spare his blushes?

He climbed out of bed, pulled on his boxer shorts, grabbed the rest of his clothes—and then made the mistake of glancing back at the bed. She looked so cute, lying there. Warm and sweet. He almost dropped his clothes back on the floor and climbed back in beside her again. Especially as he remembered last night so clearly. Touching her. Tasting her. The look of sheer pleasure in her eyes just before she'd fallen apart. The soft little cry she'd made when she'd climaxed in his arms.

No, no and absolutely no.

Common sense won—just—and he managed to get back to his own room without bumping into anyone in the corridor.

Showering helped to restore a little more of his common sense, once he'd turned the temperature of the water right down. Once he'd dressed, he stripped the bed, threw everything into his case, and knocked on Bella's door.

'Come in,' she called.

She was just closing the lid of her suitcase, and she was wearing a strappy top and the shortest pair of denim cut-offs he'd ever seen. Her legs went on for ever. And his tongue felt as if it was glued to the roof of his mouth.

It grew even worse when she gave a little wiggle. Her bottom had the most perfect curve, and it made him want to touch her again.

'Is this ditzy enough?' she asked with a grin, seemingly oblivious to the desire coursing through him.

'Uh—yeah.' And now he sounded like a total troglodyte. He didn't want her to guess the effect she had on him, particularly as he knew she wasn't doing it deliberately. Bella wasn't a game-player. 'I need some coffee,' he gabbled wildly. 'You know I'm not a morning person.'

'Coffee sounds good. Would you mind, um, showing me where I can make some?'

'There's probably already a pot on the go downstairs.'

Though now they had to face his family at the breakfast table. Please don't let any of them start asking questions about where he and Bella had disappeared to last night, he begged silently.

When he ushered Bella into the kitchen, his brothers and their partners were all sitting there, along with Sophia in her high chair; his mother was bustling around and his father was deep in the Sunday newspapers. He narrowed his eyes at them all in warning that they were absolutely not to say a single word, and to his relief they actually went along with him, saying nothing more awkward to her than a cheerful, 'Good morning.'

Without another word, he pulled out a chair at the table for Bella, then sat down next to her.

'Would you like tea or coffee?' Libby asked, coming over to them.

'Coffee, please,' Bella said. 'Can I do anything to help?'

'No, sweetie, it's fine. Bacon sandwich? I'm just about to do another batch.'

'Yes, please.' Bella smiled. 'Bacon and sandwich have to be the two most perfect words for a Sunday morning.'

'And coffee,' Nigel added with a smile. 'Don't forget coffee. Especially where Hugh's concerned.'

'I reckon it'll be another twenty minutes before we get a civil word out of our Hugh,' Julian teased.

'And the rest! He only ever grunts before midday,' Alastair added. 'Even *with* coffee.'

'Now, now, children,' Libby said, mock-warning.

Bella was really enjoying the byplay between Hugh and his brothers. She missed chatting in the kitchen with her mum and her sister on Sunday morning, when her dad would be deep in the Sunday papers in the living room and they would talk about anything and everything— from films to books to seriously girly stuff that would make her dad squirm.

Then her smile faded. If any of her family knew what had happened last night… Well. Nobody would be surprised. If there was a way to mess things up, Bella would be the one to find it. But she and Hugh had agreed that they'd act as if last night hadn't happened.

She just hoped that he meant it.

The kitchen was amazing, a huge room with cream cupboards and tiled floors, with an Aga and an island workstation as well as the breakfast area with the massive table looking out onto the garden. There were comfortable-looking dog beds next to the Aga, but Bella had already worked out that the Labrador, the Westie and the spaniel were all sitting under the table, waiting patiently for treats to be sneaked down to them. 'Your kitchen's really lovely, Libby,' she said.

'Thank you,' Libby replied, putting a plate of bacon sandwiches onto the table. 'Has Hugh shown you the rest of the house yet?'

Only the orangery. And Bella had to fight to prevent the blush that threatened to betray her. 'Not yet,' she said.

'I promised I'd do that before we go out for our walk,' Hugh drawled.

'Make sure you do,' Libby said.

Bella noticed that little Sophia was fussing in her high chair; both Poppy and Julian looked exhausted, and she guessed that Sophia had slept badly during the night, meaning that so had her parents. 'Can I give her a cuddle?' Bella asked.

Poppy looked torn between wariness and gratitude.

'One of my friends does music classes for babies and toddlers,' Bella said. 'So I know a few things that might help distract her—then you might be able to have your breakfast in peace.'

'You haven't had your own breakfast yet,' Poppy said.

'I'll be fine.' Bella shrugged and smiled. 'So can I?'

Poppy smiled back at her. 'Thank you.'

Bella didn't quite dare look at Hugh as she scooped Sophia out of the high chair and then settled the baby on her lap. But Sophia clearly enjoyed being bounced to 'Humpty Dumpty' and 'Row, Row, Row Your Boat' and the other nursery songs Bella could remember, and she was gurgling with delight when Julian picked her up from Bella's lap again.

'Eat your bacon sandwich before it gets cold,' he said, patting her shoulder. 'And thank you for cheering up Miss Grumpy here.'

'Any time,' Bella said with a smile.

'Can I help with the washing up?' Bella asked when she'd finished her sandwich.

Libby shook her head. 'No, sweetie. Thank you for the offer, but it's fine.'

'The kitchen is Ma's domain,' Nigel explained.

'My mum's the same, except we all pitch in and help when we have family over for lunch, because it's really not fair to make someone peel all the veg on their own,' Bella said.

'Well, if you really want to, you can help me with the veg,' Libby conceded. 'But let Hugh show you round first.'

'Hint taken,' Hugh said and stood up. 'Come on, Bella.'

She took his hand and let him lead her out of the kitchen.

He dropped her hand again, the minute they were out of sight. 'Guided tour,' he said, and proceeded to whisk her through the house. The house was glorious, with mullioned windows upstairs and floor-to-ceiling windows downstairs.

'Hugh,' she said when he'd taken her swiftly through the library, not even letting her browse a single shelf in the acres of shelving.

'What?'

'What did I do wrong?' she asked.

'Nothing.' But his voice was clipped.

She sighed. 'Was it because I cuddled the baby? I *like* babies, Hugh. And I like your family.'

'You're meant to be unsuitable,' he reminded her.

'Even unsuitable girlfriends can like babies.'

'Hmm,' he said. 'Drawing room.' There were com-

fortable chairs and amazing artwork on the walls, and a
den with a state of the art television and music system.

'Dining room.'

She'd already seen this the previous day, and the ballroom—though it was much less intimidating now it was
empty. She was almost tempted to ask him to play something for her on the piano, something soft and gentle for
a Sunday morning, but there was an odd expression on
his face and she didn't quite dare.

So much for the Vegas principle. He was clearly finding it hard to ignore what had happened between them.

And that was probably why he didn't show her the
orangery in daylight. It would've been too much of a re-
minder of how reckless they'd been.

'Do you want your family to think we've had a fight?'
she asked when he'd finished the tour and was leading
her back to the kitchen.

'Fight? Oh.' The penny clearly dropped, and he took
her hand again.

Except it felt grudging.

Considering that *he'd* been the one to come up with
the idea of the unsuitable girlfriend in the first place,
Bella wanted to shake him by the scruff of his neck.
'You have to be the most difficult man in the universe,'
she muttered.

He didn't disagree with her. And she had the nasty
feeling that she was going to be looking for another job,
pretty soon. She just hoped that Tarquin would give her
a decent reference—she certainly wasn't going to ask
Hugh. And she wasn't telling Grace about any of this.
So much for standing on her own two feet and getting
her life in shape. She'd just messed up again. Big time.

In the kitchen, everyone was still drinking coffee.

Libby looked at her shoes. 'You need to borrow some wellingtons, Bella, or you'll risk ruining those lovely shoes.'

'I guess they're probably not that suitable for a walk in the garden,' she said, playing Miss Ditzy—though her heart really wasn't in this any more.

'Hugh will find you something in the boot room,' Oliver said.

She blinked. 'You have a room just for *boots*?' Hugh hadn't shown her that.

'It's for boots, coats and muddy dogs to dry off in,' Hugh explained.

The boot room turned out to be just off the kitchen. The room had a stone chequered floor that reminded Bella a bit of the orangery, teamed with white tongue and groove panelling on the cabinets. There were shelves of wellington boots, pegs for coats, and a couple of wicker picnic baskets on shelves; there were also a washing machine and tumble dryer, and she guessed that there would be an iron and ironing board in one of the cupboards.

Hugh checked her shoe size and came up with a pair of green wellington boots and an ancient waxed jacket that was too big for her. 'You'll need socks,' he said, and rummaged in one of the wicker baskets for an old but clean pair of what looked like rugby socks.

And at least borrowing a jacket meant she had pockets to shove her hands into and she wouldn't have the temptation of being hand-in-hand with Hugh—or the awkwardness if she tried to hold his hand and he rejected her, which she thought would be the most likely outcome.

Hugh's brothers and their partners all joined them on the walk, along with Sophia in her pushchair, and the dogs romped along happily beside them.

'So we're going for a walk in the nearby woods or something?' she asked.

Hugh nodded. 'They're part of the estate.'

Well, of course a huge manor house like this would come with an estate rather than just a garden. How stupid of her not to think of that before.

But her awkwardness turned to delight when they walked through the narrow paths in the woods and she could see bluebells everywhere. 'That's gorgeous!'

'It's still a bit early for them yet,' Hugh said, 'but they're like a blue haze when they're fully out.'

'A real bluebell carpet—how lovely,' she said. It made her itch to sit out here with a pad of cartridge paper and a box of watercolours. 'I love the colour of new leaves, that really bright lime-green that means spring's really here.'

'Yeah.'

Somehow, Hugh was holding her hand again, and it sent a shiver of pure desire through her.

He met her gaze. 'I'm not coming on to you,' he said in a low voice. 'Everyone will expect me to hold my girl-friend's hand.'

'Of course,' she said, but she had to swallow her disappointment. Which was ridiculous in any case. She didn't want a relationship and she didn't want to mess up her job. Hugh was off limits and this was simply a bit of play-acting for his family's benefit. They'd agreed. And the fact that he was holding her hand simply meant that the bluebells had just got rid of his Monday morning-itis, which was actually more like *every* morning-itis.

Back at the house, the others all disappeared to sort out various things, and Hugh's father called him to come and help with something. Feeling a bit like a spare part,

Bella went in search of Libby in the kitchen. 'I promised to help you with the vegetables.'

'You really don't have to,' Libby said. 'You're a guest.'

'Even so,' Bella said. 'Is that beef I smell roasting?'

'Yes.'

'I could make the Yorkshire puddings, if you like.' She laughed. 'I admit I'm a terrible cook, but I'm actually quite good at cupcakes, pancakes and Yorkshire puddings. I guess it's because they're light and fluffy, like me.'

Libby gave her look as if to say that she knew there was much more to Bella than that, or Hugh wouldn't be dating her. 'You're playing a part, this weekend, aren't you?'

Uh-oh. She hadn't expected Libby to call her on it. 'A part?' Bella asked, trying not to panic. 'What makes you say that?'

'Because the real you keeps shining through. The way you brought me my favourite chocolates, the way you looked after Lavinia yesterday afternoon, the way you drew those pictures for everyone, the way you haven't minded a muddy dog draped all over you, the way you sat and cuddled Sophia this morning during breakfast and sang nursery songs to her.' Libby ticked them off on her fingers. 'If you were the dreadful airhead that you and Hugh clearly want us all to think you are, I'm not so sure you would've done any of that.'

There was no way she could keep up the pretence any more. 'Busted, I guess. But please don't tell Hugh you know.'

'I won't,' Libby said softly. 'But what I don't understand is why you both feel that you have to play a part.'

'I did tell him Plan B would be better,' Bella said with a rueful smile.

Libby's frown deepened. 'What's Plan B?'

Bella held up both hands in a surrender gesture. 'Just ignore me. I'm rambling.'

'No, I think this is something I need to know,' Libby said.

Bella bit her lip. 'Please, please don't shoot the messenger, because you've all been so kind and I don't want to be rude and ungrateful. Even though I've already been rude and obnoxious.'

'Now you're really worrying me,' Libby said. 'What's plan B?'

'To tell you the truth about his job and make you see how he feels. Hugh isn't a stockbroker at heart,' Bella said, 'he's a music producer. He loves his job and he's really, really good at it. I really don't mean to be rude or to offend you, but he seems to believe that you all want him to toe the line—to sell Insurgo Records to the highest bidder and join the family firm instead. If he does that, you're going to break his heart and his spirit. He'd hate it so much and he'd spend all his time wishing he was somewhere else. And then he might grow to resent you all instead of loving you like he does now.'

Libby was silent for so long that Bella thought she'd gone too far.

'Mrs Moncrieff? Libby?' she asked anxiously.

Libby's eyes were glistening with tears. 'Those were very wise words,' she said softly. 'And they came from the heart.'

Hugh was halfway down the corridor to the kitchen when he heard his mother ask, 'So are you his real girlfriend pretending to be his fake girlfriend?'

What?

Oh, no. He knew his mother was perceptive. He needed to go in and head her off. Or had Bella already caved in and told her the truth?

To his horror, he heard Bella say, 'That all sounds so complicated. But I was telling you the truth when I said I'm the designer at Insurgo.'

Oh, hell. She *had* caved in. She'd blown their cover completely. And he was shocked by how hurt and disappointed he was. He'd been telling himself that Bella wasn't like Jessie—and yet she'd let him down, too. She'd promised to play a part and she'd gone back on her word. Betrayed his trust. Ratted him out to his mother, so his subterfuge was well and truly uncovered. So much for thinking that she was different. Obviously his judgement was still way off.

'That,' Libby said, 'figures.'

'What does?' Bella asked.

Hugh went cold. Please don't let his mother start talking about Jessie. He only realised he was holding his breath when Libby said, 'If he hasn't told you, I won't break his confidence.'

'That's not very fair, given that I've just done that,' Bella said.

She'd even admitted what she'd done. And it made him feel sick. How far had she gone?

He strode into the kitchen. 'Breaking my confidence?' he asked.

Bella went white. 'Hugh. I didn't know you were there.'

'Obviously.' He shook his head in disgust. 'Well, thanks a bunch. I guess that'll teach me to trust you. So do you blab Insurgo's business all over social media, too, the same way you've just blabbed my personal business to my mother?'

'Hugh, that's not fair,' Libby said. 'She was trying to help.'

'She was gossiping about me.' And that hurt.

'I wasn't gossiping at all,' Bella said. 'Right now, I want to tip this Yorkshire pudding batter all over your stupid head. But I'm not going to waste food and put your mum in an awkward position. Instead I'm going to walk outside in the garden, in this stupid outfit I found to fit your even more stupid idea. And *you*,' she said, walking over to him and stabbing her finger into his chest, 'are going to sit down with your mum and talk. Really talk.'

He was too taken aback to say anything. Not that he could've got a word in edgeways, because Bella was on a roll.

'You're going to tell her how you feel about your business and how it's not just your job, it's your passion, and for you it's like breathing. And you're going to tell her that you're great at business and you don't take unnecessary risks—that you save being a total idiot for the other bits of your life. You three,' she added to the dogs, 'you're coming with me and we're going to find some tennis balls, and I'm going to pretend they're Hugh's head and kick them as hard as I can.'

'Bella—' he began, knowing that he needed to apologise.

'No. Talk to your mum,' she said. 'Right now, I don't want to talk to you. I'm going out with the dogs.'

'Take whatever you need from the boot room, love,' Libby said. 'And I'll shout at him for you.'

Bella shook her head. 'I'd much rather you listened to him,' she said softly. 'Even though right at this moment I don't like him very much, I respect him when it comes to business—and I think you both need to listen to each other.' And she walked quietly out of the kitchen, followed by the dogs.

Hugh found himself talking—*really* talking—to his mother about the most important thing in his life. And she listened. Understood. Just as he could now see that the worrying and fussing were driven by love rather than a need to make him toe a family line that didn't actually exist.

Without Bella's intervention, this would never have happened, and he knew it.

When he'd finished, Libby said, 'You owe that girl—'

'—a huge apology,' he cut in. 'I know.'

She hugged him. 'You're my youngest son, Hugh, and I love you, but I don't like you very much today.'

'I don't like myself very much, either,' he admitted.

'She isn't Jessie,' Libby said softly.

'I know.' Jessie would never have offered to help prepare the vegetables. Yes, musicians had to look after their hands, because an accidental cut or burn would affect their ability to play an instrument—but Jessie wouldn't have offered to do something that didn't risk her hands, either. She wouldn't have played with Sophia. He knew that his family hadn't taken to her—they'd been polite but reserved. But everyone had instantly warmed to Bella, from his great-aunt to his brothers and even his father. 'I need to go and talk to her.'

'Be nice,' Libby said softly. 'She's got a good heart. She didn't break your trust. She found a better way to deal with things than any of us did.'

Hugh hugged his mother back. 'I know.' And he'd messed this up. Big time.

He went outside to find Bella. She looked as if she'd

been crying, and he felt a total heel. How could he have been so unkind to her?

'Bella. I'm sorry,' he said.

'Hmm.' She didn't look in the slightest bit mollified by his apology.

'You were right and I was wrong.'

She folded her arms. 'That's rather stating the obvious.'

'And I'm sorry I was obnoxious to you. I shouldn't have said any of that.'

'Also stating the obvious,' she said.

'I can't even blame it on Monday morning-itis.' He sighed. 'How do I make it up to you?'

'You've made it clear that you don't trust me. So, actually, I don't think you can,' she said.

He blew out a breath. 'I don't have a clue what to say or what to do. Only that I'm sorry for hurting you. And, without you, I don't think my family would ever have understood what Insurgo means to me. And I wouldn't have understood how they really feel, either. I appreciate that.'

She shrugged. 'Even so, I'm not your personal punch-bag. Hugh, I don't enjoy people lashing out at me. I was only playing Miss Ditzy because you asked me to. I'm not an actress. Your mum saw right through the whole thing. And I did tell you it was a stupid idea.'

'You were right,' he said again. 'I know you probably want to be a million miles away from here right now, so if you want me to drive you straight home, then I'll do it. But I think my family would like you to stay for lunch. They like you. And I mean they like the *real* Bella Faraday,' he clarified. 'The one who looks out for elderly aunts, cuddles babies, plays ball with the dogs, is an amazing artist and brings out the best in everyone. The woman who really is the life and soul of the party— because I've never seen my entire family get up on the dance floor before you came along.'

Her eyes sparkled with tears; he brushed away the single one that spilled over her lashes.

'They don't hate me for lying to them?' she whispered.

'No. They really, really like you.' And so did he. Though now wasn't the time to say so. After the way he'd hurt her, she wouldn't believe him—and he couldn't blame her.

'Come and have lunch,' he said.

'For your mum's sake. Not yours.'

'I know,' he said softly. 'And thank you.'

Although Bella didn't say much to him once they were back in the house, she sparkled all the way through Sunday lunch. She insisted on helping to clear things away and on cuddling Sophia again when his niece had another fit of the grumps. And when his family said goodbye to her, it was with a warm, heartfelt hug rather than the formal handshakes they'd always given Jessie.

'Come back soon,' Libby said. 'And I mean *really* soon. You have to see the bluebells when they're at their best.'

'I'd love to,' Bella said, hugging her back. 'Thank you so much for having me.'

His brothers and their partners all got hugs, too, along with the baby. And so did his father, who then shocked Hugh immensely by saying, 'Come and paint the bluebells for my study, and I'll cook you my famous chicken biryani.'

Since when had his father ever cooked? Let alone something as exotic as biryani?

Hugh was so stunned that he didn't say a word until they were halfway home. And then it was only because Bella was the one to start the conversation.

'I think we need to talk,' she said carefully.

'Talk?'

She took a deep breath. 'I'm sorry I messed up your plans. If you want me to resign and go quietly from Insurgo, I'll accept that and write you an official resignation letter as soon as we're back in London.'

'No, that's not fair.' And he didn't want her to leave.

'You asked me to play your unsuitable girlfriend, and I didn't do it right.'

'I also told you to be yourself,' he said. 'And you were. Though I don't get how you do it.'

'How I do what?' she asked, sounding confused.

'Fit in so effortlessly. When you joined Insurgo, within a couple of days it was as if you'd been one of the team right from the start. And my family. They took to you like they never did to—' He stopped abruptly.

'Never did to whom?' she asked softly.

'Never mind.'

'The girl who broke your heart? The one you worked with?'

He gave her a sidelong glance. 'Fishing, Bella?'

'No—but I can hardly ask you straight out about it, can I? You're not exactly approachable.'

'My past isn't any of your—' he began, then stopped, knowing that he was being completely unfair to her. 'Sorry. That was rude and unkind. Especially as you've just given up your whole weekend to do me a favour, and I've already treated you badly. I apologise unreservedly. And you have the right to stamp all over me in spike heels.'

'Spike heels?'

'Your "three strikes and you're out" rule. I've broken that several times.'

'That's bravado,' Bella said, sounding sad. 'I don't really stomp on people.' And he felt even guiltier when she added, 'Besides, you're right. Your past isn't any of my business.' She sighed. 'Did you hear everything I said to your mum?'

'Only from when she asked you if you were my real girlfriend pretending to be my pretend girlfriend.' He gave her another swift look. Guilt was written all over her face. 'Is there more I should know about?'

'I told her that you're Insurgo's heart—and joining the family firm would break your spirit and make you resent them instead of loving them and being exasperated by them as you do now.'

If Hugh hadn't been driving, he would've closed his eyes in horror. 'We never talk about that sort of stuff.'

'I think you might do, in future,' Bella said softly. 'But, as I said earlier, I understand if you want me to resign.'

'Right now,' Hugh said, 'I think the best thing would be if neither of us said another word until we get back to London.'

'OK,' Bella said, and lapsed into silence.

Which made Hugh feel even more mean and guilty. He knew she'd said everything with the best of intentions. But his head was in a whirl. Bella Faraday knocked him seriously off balance, and he didn't trust himself to say what he really meant. He wasn't even sure what he really felt, other than being completely mixed up, so it was better to say nothing.

It didn't help that he could still smell her perfume, and

that made him remember kissing her in the orangery last night. That kiss—and what had happened afterwards—was something he really couldn't dare to repeat. So it was better to put a little bit of metaphorical distance between them. Wasn't it?

Finally he pulled up in the road outside her flat. 'I'll see you to your door.'

'There's no need,' Bella said. 'Thank you for the lift. And I won't ask you in. Not because I'm being rude, but because I'm sure you're busy. And, tomorrow morning, when we're back in the office, this weekend never happened.'

'Agreed,' he said.

Even though he didn't see her to the door, Hugh waited until she'd closed her front door behind her before he drove away. That was the very least he could do. And as for the damage to their working relationship... He'd better hope that he could fix it. Because the only way he could keep Bella in his life was as a colleague—and he didn't want to lose her.

What a weekend, Bella thought as she closed the front door behind her.

She changed swiftly into a more comfortable—not to mention demure—pair of jeans and a normal T-shirt, and bustled about sorting out things in her flat. There was a message on her phone from Grace.

Give me a ring when you're back and let me know how it went xxx

Yeah, right. Bella rolled her eyes. She could hardly admit to her sister what she'd done: slept with her boss, gone completely off brief, interfered and told his mother the truth, and then had a huge row with Hugh. Even though he'd apologised, she still hated the fact that he thought he couldn't trust her. Maybe his ex had broken his ability to trust, the way Kirk had broken hers; but it still hurt that he could think of her in that way. Did he not know her at all?

So she left it until late in the evening to text a reply to Grace: *Just got back.* That was stretching a point, but it was only a tiny fib. *Too late to call.* That bit was true. *All fine.* That bit might not be true. But she hoped that Grace wouldn't push her for more details—and that things would be OK in the office tomorrow. That she and Hugh could pretend that nothing had ever happened. Because, otherwise, she'd be looking for another job.

And, if she left Insurgo, it wasn't just the job she'd miss.

CHAPTER SEVEN

ON MONDAY MORNING, Bella was slightly nervous as she walked in to the Insurgo offices. She bought a double-shot cappuccino from the café downstairs to give her courage. Would Hugh be the same with her as he usually was, or would he avoid her? Would he be more difficult than he usually was on Monday mornings?

But he wasn't in the office. He'd left Tarquin a message to say that he was in a meeting across town and probably wouldn't make it in to the office until very late that day, if at all. Bella wasn't sure if she was more relieved at not having to face him or disappointed at missing him; though she knew that she couldn't let anyone guess how she was feeling. Nobody knew she'd been in Oxfordshire with Hugh, and it had to stay that way. As far as everyone at the Insurgo offices was concerned, he was the boss and she was simply the graphic designer. Full stop.

By Wednesday, Hugh knew that he had to show his face in the office or Tarquin would start working things out for himself. But he wasn't sure if he could do what Bella had suggested and work on the Vegas principle.

On paper, it was easy. What had happened in Oxfordshire should stay in Oxfordshire.

The problem was, he could still remember what it felt like to wake up wrapped round her. And, worse still, he wanted to do it again.

But he couldn't see a way of making this work. He already knew that from his experience with Jessie. Even though Bella wasn't anything like Jessie, the equation was the same: business plus relationship equals disaster.

So either he dated her and she left the company—which wouldn't be good for Insurgo, because she was a great designer—or she stayed in her job and he'd have to keep a lid on his feelings. It made business sense for it to be the latter. Plus he was used to keeping a lid on his feelings.

But that had been before Bella Faraday exploded into his life. Before he'd taken her home as his 'unsuitable' girlfriend. Before she'd turned his world upside down.

Bella was aware of every time Hugh walked into the room, even when her back was to the door.

She looked up several times from her work when he was in the main office, talking to Tarquin, and caught his eye. He looked away again almost immediately. And, because Hugh was so good at being impassive, she didn't have a clue what he was thinking.

Was he thinking about what had happened between them? Did he feel the same pull, the same awareness, as she did? Or was he regretting every single moment?

She was half tempted to text him and suggest that they talked. But that would be needy and pathetic, and that wasn't who she was. She'd got through Kirk's betrayal, and this situation with Hugh wasn't anywhere near that on the scale of awfulness.

Things would all settle down, soon enough. She

would get to the stage where she could look at Hugh without remembering how it had felt when he'd touched her and kissed her. Where she could look at him without wanting him to kiss her again. It would just take a bit of time, that was all. Until then, she'd just have to keep a lid on her feelings. This wasn't appropriate, and she wasn't in a position where she dared do anything to jeopardise her job.

Hugh sat in front of his computer with his elbows resting on the desk and his chin propped in his hands. This was ridiculous. He never, ever let anything distract his focus from his work.

But he couldn't stop thinking about Bella.

Maybe he should call her. Text her. Tell her he'd like to change his mind about the Vegas principle and see her now they were back in London. Ask her out to dinner or to a show.

But then things would start to get complicated in the office, and he didn't want that. He knew that keeping his distance from her was the sensible thing to do.

All the same, he was antsy. He couldn't settle to anything. And he knew it was making him snappy with everyone.

On the Thursday, he was glad that one of his artists was in the studio in the basement, recording an album. It gave him an excuse to stay out of the office and focus on producing the music—the part of his job he loved most. That would keep his head too busy to let him think about Bella Faraday.

And he actually managed it...until lunchtime, when Tarquin brought Bella down to meet the band and talk about the cover art concept.

She'd changed her hair colour again, Hugh noticed. Today she was brunette. It was a huge change from the almost fire-engine-red she'd sported in Oxfordshire, but it suited her and it brought out the depths of her eyes. It made her look seriously pretty.

How he wanted to twirl the ends of her hair round his fingers. Feel how soft and silky it was. And then touch his mouth to hers...

What made it worse was that she was dressed in faded jeans which hugged her curves, and spike-heeled ankle boots. She'd teamed it with a black T-shirt with the Insurgo logo on the front, clearly going for the rock chick look. And she carried it off beautifully.

He wasn't surprised that she charmed the band as quickly as she'd charmed his family. Just by being herself: bright, vivacious Bella with her ready laugh, and the way she touched people's hands or arms or shoulders when she spoke. She was very tactile; and yet she didn't make you feel as if she'd invaded your personal space. It felt natural. Easy.

Hugh caught her eye. Was it his imagination, or was there the faintest blush in her cheeks as she looked at him? Probably his imagination, he decided, because she was totally professional and almost cool with him. Clearly she didn't have a problem with the Vegas principle.

They discussed the album concept and cover with the band, and Bella made a few sketches and notes. Hugh could barely take his eyes off her hands. He remembered how they'd felt against his skin, and it made him ache.

When would he stop wanting her?

Tarquin had also organised a buffet lunch for all of them, sent down by the café on the ground floor. Being together in a more social setting would be awkward, Hugh thought, but no way could he or Bella get out of this. He hadn't said a word to Tarquin about the situation and he was pretty sure that she hadn't said anything, either, or his business partner would've had quite a lot to say about it.

Well, they'd just have to roll with it and pretend that everything was normal. Even though it wasn't.

He noticed that Jet, the band's lead singer, was flirting with Bella during lunch. She wasn't encouraging him at all; she was professional and polite and made sure that she included the rest of the band in the conversation. Hugh couldn't fault her behaviour. But he really wanted to snarl at Jet and tell him to back off, because Bella wasn't available. Which would put her in an impossible situation, so he kept his tongue firmly under control.

But then he reached for the plate of sandwiches at the same time as Bella did. As his fingers brushed against hers, he felt the heat zing through him. And when his gaze caught hers, her pupils went just that little bit darker and wider. So was it the same for her, too? This crazy, raging need that sent him into a flat spin?

And just what were they going to do about this?

The more time Hugh spent with her, the more he wanted her—and this wasn't fair to either of them. But right at that moment he couldn't see a way of making things better. Not without complicating things or risking things getting a whole lot worse.

To his relief, after lunch Bella made an excuse to go back up to the office with Tarquin, which left him to concentrate on the music and the band and working on the arrangements.

Jet turned to him at the end of the next song. 'I was going to ask you—could you give me Bella's number?'

'To discuss the album cover?' Hugh asked, deliberately misunderstanding the other man. 'Just call the usual office number and someone will put you through to her.'

'No, I meant...'

'What?' Uh-oh. He really hoped that Jet hadn't picked up how short his tone was.

But the singer didn't seem fussed in the slightest. 'Dating her, man,' he said with a grin. 'I know you're dedicated to your work, Hugh, but surely even *you* have noticed how hot she is?'

Of course he'd noticed. More than noticed. 'She's my colleague,' he said crisply. 'I never mix business and relationships.'

Jet gave him a look as if to say, *more fool you*. 'So can you give me her number?'

'She might already be involved with someone.'

Jet held his gaze. 'And she might not.'

'I'll let her know you asked, and leave it up to her if she wants to call you,' Hugh said. And he seriously hoped she didn't. Even though he knew he was being a complete dog in the manger, given that he wasn't actually in a relationship with Bella. For all he knew, she might actually want to date Jet. But he'd be much happier if she didn't. 'Now, let's get back to work and go through the next song, shall we?'

Later that afternoon, when the band had left, Hugh walked back into the office. Bella was working at her desk, but he knew by the sudden tension in her shoulders that she knew he was there.

'Jet asked for your number,' he said abruptly.

Her head snapped up and she stared at him. 'Jet?'

'The lead singer of the band. You were talking to him at lunch.' And Jet had most definitely been flirting with her. Surely she'd been aware of that?

'Oh.'

'I told him to ring the office and someone would put him through, if he wants to discuss the album cover.'

'Uh-huh.'

He couldn't tell anything from her expression. Which left him with no choice; he'd have to raise the issue. 'Jet didn't want to discuss business.'

'Then what did he want?'

He gave her a speaking look. Wasn't it obvious? 'I told him that relationships and business don't mix.'

And now there was the tiniest, tiniest glint in her eyes. Amusement? Anger? Pity? He wasn't sure. There was no way he could ask without betraying himself, and until he knew what was going on in her head he didn't want her to know what he was feeling.

'Did you, now?' she drawled.

'I said I'd tell you he'd asked.'

'I might,' Bella said, 'already be committed to some-one.'

'So you might,' he said. And he had to suppress the wish that it was him.

'I'll make sure he knows that,' she said.

So she wasn't going to date the guy? He was shocked by the way it made him feel as if a massive weight had been lifted from his shoulders. 'Thank you.' But he didn't want her to realise he was glad for selfish reasons. 'I like the office to run smoothly,' he added coolly.

'Noted, Mr Moncrieff.'

And then she did something that nearly finished

him off. She moistened her lower lip with the tip of her tongue, so her lips looked as shiny as if she'd just been kissed. *Just as she'd looked when he'd kissed her.*

'Right,' he said, and left for his own office. While he still could.

Back at his desk, he rested his elbows on the table and propped his face in his hands. When was he going to stop wanting this woman? When was his common sense going to come back? He knew it wouldn't work between them. It couldn't.

Yet he still wanted her.

By the end of the next week, Hugh was near to going insane. Throwing himself into work wasn't making any difference at all. And when he was at home he actually found himself sitting down with a guitar in his hand or at the piano, something he hadn't done in a long time. There were little snatches of songs buzzing round in his head—nothing he recognised, so he knew they were his own compositions. There were bits of melodies, bits of introductions, and bits of a middle eight. None of them fitted together and none of the melodies had proper words to go with them, but Hugh knew that he was starting to write songs again.

And that worried him even more.

It had taken him a year to get over the mess that Jessie's betrayal had caused. He didn't want to leave himself open to the risk of feeling that low ever, ever again—even though part of him was glad that the music he loved so much was bubbling up inside him again, and he knew it was all due to Bella.

But this was all too complicated.

He was just going to have to get over these growing

feelings for Bella and ignore them. And ignore the hints from his parents that the bluebells were starting to look really pretty and the dogs would love to go for a run with him. They might just as well have texted him in capitals to say WE WANT TO SEE BELLA.

Well, it wasn't happening.

What happened in Oxfordshire, stayed in Oxfordshire. They'd agreed it. Their relationship had been strictly business from that Sunday afternoon onwards.

So why couldn't Bella get Hugh out of her head? Why could she still feel the warmth of his body wrapped round her? Why, every time she closed her eyes, did she remember him kissing her among the fairy lights until they were both dizzy?

'Are you OK, Bella?' Tarquin asked.

'Fine.' She smiled at him. 'Just a bit of a headache.' A headache called Hugh Moncrieff. Not that she would ever admit that to anyone at Insurgo. Since they'd been back, Hugh's cool and professional behaviour towards her had made it clear that their relationship was strictly business. And she didn't want to cause tension in the office. Even so, she couldn't help asking, 'Tarq, have you known Hugh for very long?'

'We were at school together, so yes. Why?'

'I just wondered,' she said, 'why he has this thing about not mixing business and relationships.'

'Ah. That's not my story to tell, sweet-cheeks,' Tarquin said softly. 'Why? Are you...?'

Oh, no. He hadn't guessed how she felt about Hugh, had he? 'No, no, not at all,' she fibbed hastily. 'It's just something he said when Jet from the band asked for my number.'

'OK.'

But Tarquin looked curious, and Bella wished she hadn't said anything. 'Just being nosey,' she said sweetly. 'Obviously something's happened in the past that made things difficult for everyone in the office, so he doesn't want people to get involved with people they have to work with. I get it.'

'Something like that,' Tarquin said.

But he still looked oddly at her, and she knew she had to do something to distract him. 'I'm going to do a tea and coffee run. What do you want?' Even if that did mean going upstairs to the staff kitchen and being even closer to Hugh's office, it would hopefully distract Tarquin and he wouldn't start working things out or leaping to conclusions.

'I'd love a coffee, thank you, sweetie,' Tarquin said, and to her relief the sticky moment was over.

On Friday evening, Tarquin walked into Hugh's office and tapped the face of his watch with an exaggerated motion. 'Right, you. Time to turn the computer off.'

Hugh frowned. 'Not now, Tarq. I've got a couple of things to do.'

'They can wait. We're meeting Ro, or had you forgotten?'

Roland was their other best friend from school. And both Hugh and Tarquin had been worried about him for months; their regular fortnightly meeting was their way of keeping an eye on him, under the guise of rescuing Hugh from being a total workaholic. 'I'd forgotten what today was,' Hugh admitted. He glanced at the screen. 'OK. Let me save the file and shut the computer down, and we'll go.'

* * *

Roland walked into the bar at roughly the same time they did, and raised his hand to show he'd seen them.

But although Hugh had thought this was all about keeping an eye on Roland, he was in for a surprise when Tarquin turned to him after ordering two beers and a mineral water for Roland.

'All righty. You're being more of a nightmare than usual in the office, Hugh. I'm pretty sure it's got something to do with your brother's engagement party—and, as I haven't been able to get it out of you, Ro's going to do the thumbscrews.'

Roland spread his hands. 'That pretty much sums it up. So you can tell us now, or we can nag you until you tell us. Your choice, but I'd advise saving all the drag of us droning on at you and just telling us.'

Hugh raked a hand through his hair. 'Nothing's wrong.'

'Or,' Roland suggested, 'I could call your mother and tell her that Tarq and I are worried about you. She'll tell us what you're not saying.'

Which was what Hugh and Tarquin had done to Roland, the previous year, out of sheer desperation. It had worked, but they'd had an unspoken pact since then that calling any of their mothers was off limits.

'No. *Don't* call Ma. Please.' Hugh had been avoiding his mother's calls, too, returning her answering machine messages with a brief text to say he was up to his eyes at work and would call her soon. If his two best friends tag-teamed her and she told them the information he'd been keeping back, he wouldn't stand a chance. He put his hands up in a gesture of surrender. 'OK. I'll talk.' At least then maybe he could do some damage limitation.

Tarquin handed him a beer and gestured to one of the quieter tables in the corner.

They really weren't going to let him off this, were they? He suppressed a sigh and went to sit down.

'Tell us, sweet-cheeks,' Tarquin said. 'What happened at Nigel's party?'

Hugh blew out a breath. 'I thought I was being so clever. I took someone with me. A pretend girlfriend. Someone unsuitable. The idea was that they'd all be so horrified by her that they'd be glad when I told them it was all over—and then they'd back off.'

Tarquin and Roland exchanged a glance. 'But?' Tarquin asked.

Hugh grimaced. 'They saw through it. And they liked her. A lot.'

'Hmm. If you liked her enough to ask for her help, and she liked you enough to go along with it, and your family all liked her, then it sounds to me as if you're looking at this from completely the wrong direction,' Roland said. 'Why don't you just date the girl properly?'

'You know why,' Hugh said. 'After Jessie, there's no way I'm getting involved with anyone again. Nothing serious. I'm concentrating on the business. That's how I like my life.'

'Not all women are like Jessie,' Tarquin said. 'There's no reason why you can't try again with someone else.'

Hugh folded his arms. 'I *know* not all women are like Jessie. But I don't trust my own judgement any more. I was stupid enough to let her fool me, so what's to say I won't make the same mistake again?'

'Because you're too bright to do that,' Tarquin said. 'Think about it. You earned a first class degree.'

'Plus you own the hottest indie record label in the

country and the business is going from strength to strength,' Roland said.

It was now. Thanks to a lot of hard work—and Roland's investment. But Hugh knew just how much damage had been done to his business by letting his heart rule his head over Jessie.

'Tarq has a point,' Roland continued. 'It's been a while. Surely you're lonely?'

Yes. He was. And he wanted Bella. Hugh's temper flared. 'That's rich, coming from you.'

'That's a different kettle of fish altogether,' Roland said, his voice very quiet.

Hugh saw the emptiness in his best friend's eyes and flinched. 'Ro, I'm sorry—that was way, way below the belt. I apologise unreservedly. I shouldn't have said that.' Roland was single, but not from choice; his wife had died in a car crash eighteen months ago, and he was still mourning her. Some well-meaning friends had tried matchmaking over the last few months, but every attempt had failed spectacularly.

'Apology accepted.' But Roland's voice was completely neutral, and Hugh knew he'd overstepped the mark. Big time. Exactly the way he'd lashed out at Bella—and for exactly the same reason.

The only way he could think of to make amends was to tell the truth. Well, some of it. 'I *am* sorry, Ro. This whole thing makes me antsy, and I shouldn't have taken it out on you. I'm just as horrible at work, and...' He shrugged. 'I hate being like it. Everyone else hates it just as much. But I don't seem to be able to stop myself.'

Tarquin patted his arm. 'You're in Monday morning mode. We get it. Now spill.'

'I like her. A lot. And it scares me stupid,' he admitted. 'The way I feel about her is like nothing else I've ever known. Not even Jessie. I just can't get her out of my head.'

'Are you going to tell us anything about her?' Roland asked.

Hugh squirmed. How could he do this without giving away too much? 'She's bright, she's funny, and she makes me feel as if the world's full of sunshine.'

'Which sounds perfect. So why aren't you dating her officially?' Tarquin asked.

'It's complicated,' Hugh hedged.

'Complicated how?' Roland asked.

Hugh put his face in his hands. There was no way out of this, any more. He was going to have to bite the bullet. 'Because she works for Insurgo,' he muttered. '*Now* do you get why it's a problem?'

Tarquin groaned. 'No. Please. Not Bella. Tell me you didn't take Bella with you to Oxfordshire.'

'Who's Bella?' Roland asked, looking mystified. 'And why would it be so bad if Hugh was with her?'

'Bella's our new designer,' Tarquin explained. 'She's really good at her job, and she makes everyone in the office laugh for all the right reasons. She fitted in from the moment she walked in to Insurgo. She's adorable. If I was straight, I'd be tempted to ask her to marry me. Which gives you an idea of just how great she is.' He looked at Hugh, unsmiling. 'All righty. Bottom line. How does she feel about you?'

'I don't know.' Hugh looked away.

Tarquin groaned. 'I've got a bad feeling about this. I thought she'd been a bit wary of you in the office, this last week or so. And you've been grumpier than usual. I assumed it was because of your family—but it's not, is it?'

'Bella Faraday and I are not an item,' Hugh said calmly. 'Don't worry, Tarq. It'll be absolutely fine. Things will settle down. We talked about it.'

'Did you tell her about Jessie?' Roland asked.

'No. The subject didn't come up.' Which was a big fat lie. The subject *had* come up, but his family hadn't told her quite enough for her to work it out for herself, and Hugh had refused flatly to discuss it. He'd even been rude to Bella when she'd asked. Unkind. Unfair.

Tarquin rolled his eyes. 'Great. So now I'm going to have to scour London for a new designer—one as good as she is and who'll fit in as quickly as she has. Which is practically impossible. You *idiot*. I could shake you until your teeth rattle.'

'It's fine,' Hugh repeated. 'She's staying. We understand each other.'

'You mean you've both said all the right words,' Roland said. 'And neither of you have said what you're really thinking.'

'Neither of us wants any complications,' Hugh insisted.

'But you complicated it anyway?' Tarquin asked dryly.

'Yes,' Hugh admitted. He told them about her dress and the curtains in the ballroom, making them both laugh. 'And I sang with her.'

His best friends both went still. 'She sings?' Roland asked, his voice very soft.

'Not professionally,' Hugh said. 'Tarq already told you that she's a graphic artist. She really loves what she does. She doesn't want to be a pop star.'

'Ro, this isn't a re-run of the Jessie situation,' Tarquin said. 'Bella's nothing like Jessie at all. If someone came and offered her ten times her salary to work for them instead of for Hugh, she'd tell them to get lost. She's loyal, she's sweet and she's utterly lovely.' He looked at Hugh. 'And you know it, too. Actually, now I think about it, she's absolutely perfect for you and she might even make you into a nicer man. Except you're such an idiot that you won't give her a chance.'

Hugh folded his arms. 'You know how I feel about the situation, and you know I'm right. Mixing business and your love life is a recipe for disaster.'

'No. Getting mixed up with Jessie was a recipe for disaster,' Roland corrected. 'How many people meet their partners at work and there's a happy ending?' He paused. 'I met Lynette at work. And, if it hadn't been for the car accident, we'd still be together now.'

Hugh patted his shoulder awkwardly. 'What happened to her was beyond awful, Ro.'

'Yeah. But,' he said, surprising Hugh, 'I've decided it's time to make the effort. Lyn wouldn't have wanted me to spend the rest of my life on my own, missing her and being lonely. She would've wanted me to live life to the full.'

'So you're going to date again? Have you actually met someone?' Tarquin asked.

'No. But I'm going to try,' Roland said. 'Jessie, on the other hand, would want you to be on your own and miserable, Hugh. Which is because she's totally self-absorbed and wants the universe to revolve round her. Are you really going to let her make the rest of your life as lonely and empty as it's been for the past year, when you've met someone you actually like and you have a chance of grabbing happiness with both hands?'

'You,' Hugh said, 'are trying to pull a guilt trip on me.'

'No,' Tarquin said. 'He's telling you that it's OK to feel let down by Jessie, but it's not OK to wallow in it. Talk to Bella. Find out how she feels about you. Then, if she feels the same way you do, just sweep her off her feet.'

Could he?

Should he?

Would it all go wrong anyway?

'Maybe,' Hugh said. 'Now, can we please change the conversation and lighten this evening up a bit?'

'Flowers for the best sister in the world,' Bella said, dumping a large bunch of flowers into Grace's arms. 'And pudding.' She swung the carrier bag from one finger, and added with a grin, 'I bought it rather than made it, so it'll be edible.'

Grace simply laughed. 'Oh, Bel. You're going to have to learn to cook, one day, you know.'

'No, I won't. I have an excellent plan. I'm going to win a million on the lottery and have a housekeeper,' Bella retorted.

'In your dreams,' Grace teased back. 'Come and sit down. The kettle's on.'

'Just what I wanted to hear. So how's the flat-hunting going?' Bella asked.

Grace wrinkled her nose. 'I'm still looking. But when I have to leave here at the end of the week, Charlene's letting me use her spare room because her flatmate's spending a month in Australia. And that'll hopefully give me enough breathing space to find somewhere.'

'You can stay at mine, any time,' Bella said. 'I know it'll be a squeeze, but I'll never see you out on the streets, Gracie.'

Grace hugged her. 'I know. And the same goes for you.'

Bella enjoyed dinner—until Grace made them both a cappuccino and said, 'So when are you going to tell me?'

'Tell you what?' Bella asked, feigning innocence and trying frantically to work out how she could distract her sister.

'About what really happened in Oxfordshire? You've been way too quiet about it.'

Bella laced her fingers together. 'There's nothing to tell.'

Grace coughed. 'Try the truth.'

'I messed it up,' Bella confessed.

'So does that mean you're looking for another job?'

'Yes and no,' Bella hedged.

'You're not making a lot of sense.'

'I know.' Bella sighed. 'I don't know where to start.'

'Try the beginning?' Grace suggested gently.

'OK. I managed the afternoon tea bit OK, and I looked after his great-aunt when she wasn't feeling well.'

Grace frowned. 'That doesn't sound like messing up, to me.'

'It's not what an unsuitable girlfriend would do,' Bella pointed out.

'I guess—but it's what a decent person would do, and I know you, Bel. You couldn't have just left her to be unwell. So then what?'

'My dress for the cocktail party.' Bella blew out a breath. 'It turned out that the curtains in the ballroom were the same material as my dress.'

Grace put her hands up in a 'stop' gesture. 'Wait. Let me get my head round this. They have a *ballroom* in their house?'

Bella nodded. 'They live in an Elizabethan manor house—it's been used as a location for a few period dramas, Hugh said. Oh, Gracie, the house is utterly gorgeous, and his family's so lovely. Libby—his mum—

she's so like our mum. And his oldest brother and sister-in-law have the cutest baby, and they have three dogs.'

'I think I'm beginning to see what you meant about messing up,' Grace said. 'They didn't think you were unsuitable at all, did they?'

'Um—no.' Bella squirmed. 'I guess they kind of liked me.'

'Of course they liked you. Everyone who meets you likes you,' Grace said.

'Except Mrs Concrete Hair,' Bella said, referring to Grace's almost mother-in-law.

Grace laughed. 'I don't think she likes anyone. So his family are nice and you get on. Was that a problem for Hugh?'

'Possibly,' Bella said. 'We haven't exactly spoken much since we've been back.'

'It's difficult between you at work?'

'We pretty much ignore each other—unless we're in a meeting together, which isn't that often,' Bella said. 'And I'm just hoping that nobody in the office has noticed that it's a bit strained between us.'

'Maybe they haven't,' Grace said. 'So—back to your dress. What happened?'

'I brazened it out,' Bella said. 'I said I hadn't cut it from their curtains because they weren't the von Trapps—and then I sang "Do Re Mi".'

Grace laughed. 'That's *so* you, and I bet everyone joined in.'

'No. It was a bit awkward. And then Hugh sang "Edelweiss".' She bit her lip. 'That's something else odd, Gracie. The band his brother booked for the party was late, so Hugh played the piano until they turned up. He's really talented. And he has a gorgeous voice. I can't understand why he doesn't release records as well as produce them—and his brother said something about knowing why Hugh doesn't sing or play in public. His mother kind of let something slip, too. And Tarquin in the office, this week... I was subtle when I asked.'

Grace laughed. 'Bel, you don't do subtle.'

'Subtle for *me*, then.' She frowned. 'I might be putting two and two together and making ten, but I think Hugh fell for someone he worked with and it went pear-shaped.'

'Have you asked him about it?'

'Sort of—and he said it was none of my business. Which is quite right,' Bella added hastily, seeing Grace's eyes narrow in annoyance. 'It was rude of me to ask. And I wasn't subtle when I asked him. Anyway, we danced together. And he sneaked me off to the orangery—Gracie, it was the most romantic place ever, just the two of us and the darkness outside and fairy lights wrapped round the base of the orange trees, and he k—' She stopped, realising that maybe she shouldn't have admitted that much.

But Grace had clearly realised anyway. 'He kissed you?' she asked softly.

There was no point in trying to deny it. Especially as Grace was sensible enough to help her work out how to deal with it, and her sister could only do that if Bella told her the truth. She nodded. 'And it was like seeing stars— it's never been like that for me before.'

'Me, neither,' Grace said, sounding wistful. Then she frowned. '*Just* kissing?'

Bella winced. 'No. But we took precautions. And the next morning we agreed it'd be like the Vegas principle— what happened there, stayed there.'

'Uh-huh,' Grace said. 'So what's the situation now?'

'I don't really know,' Bella admitted. 'I like him, Gracie. I mean *really* like him. Which is crazy. We've only known each other for a few weeks. And yet in some ways I feel I've known him for ever. He's a good man. Look at the way he rescued us. And I know from talking to some of the artists that he's gone way beyond the call of duty for them. He's one of the good guys. He'd never do anything like what Kirk did.'

'Not if he wanted to keep all his bits intact, he wouldn't,' Grace said crisply.

Bella gave her sister a wan smile. 'I don't know what to do, Gracie. After Kirk, I don't really believe in love any more. And I don't want to mess up my job by falling for my boss, knowing that he doesn't believe in mixing work and relationships. One of the bands came in to record an album and the lead singer wanted to ask me out, and Hugh told him straight out that work and relationships don't mix.'

'Because he wants you for himself?'

That was the big question. Bella dragged in a breath. 'I don't actually know,' she said miserably. 'I don't know what to do, Gracie. I mean, I know I'm scatty and disorganised outside work and it's usually fine, but right now I feel as if I'm in the middle of a whirlwind, and it's really not very comfortable. I don't like feeling this way.'

'I think, love, you're going to have to take a risk and talk to him,' Grace said. 'If he likes you and you like him, then it's simple.'

'But what if he doesn't like me?'

'Bel, you're sweet and you're warm and you're funny and you're beautiful. What's not to like?'

'You're my sister. You're supposed to think that.' Bella folded her arms. 'And I don't know what he thinks of me.'

'For what it's worth,' Grace said, 'you've already said he's not like Kirk. And from what you said he's not like Howard, either—he was right there by your side when you sang "Do Re Mi". So it sounds to me as if he likes you.'

'And his family's definitely not like Mrs Concrete Hair and Mr Toad,' Bella added, referring to Howard's parents.

'Well, then. Talk to him. What's the worst that could happen?'

'That he turns me down and then it's too awkward to work with him,' Bella said.

'But isn't it already awkward working with him?' Grace asked.

'A bit,' Bella admitted. 'So I've been half thinking that I might need to find another job anyway.'

'And if you don't say anything, what's the worst that could happen?' Grace asked.

Bella knew that her sister wouldn't let her get away with being feeble. 'I'll always regret not talking to him and seeing if we could make a go of it. And maybe he'll meet someone else, and he'll never know how I felt about him because I was too much of a coward to try.'

'And you're not a coward, Bel. You're brave and you're honest and you're lovely,' Grace said. 'Talk to him.'

'I'll try,' Bella promised.

But would Hugh talk to her? Or would he keep himself shut off?

CHAPTER EIGHT

'ARE YOU SURE you don't want to leave this until the morning, sweet-cheeks?' Tarquin asked, the following Tuesday evening. 'It's late and you've already put in a lot of hours.'

'I'm sure,' Bella said firmly. 'It won't take me very long to get this finished and I really hate leaving things.'

'OK. Just let Hugh know when you leave, so he can lock up,' Tarquin said. 'I'll let him know you're working late so he doesn't accidentally lock you in or anything.'

A frisson went through her. So she and Hugh would be alone in the building?

Well, not completely alone—she knew that there would be people downstairs in the café—but there would be just the two of them in the office.

Maybe she could be brave and talk to him tonight...

'See you tomorrow, Tarq,' she said brightly. 'Have a nice evening.'

'You, too—and don't work too late, do you hear?'

She smiled and blew him a kiss; smiling back, Tarquin left her to it. Bella managed to concentrate on what she was doing and finished the piece of art she'd been working on all day. Once she'd turned off her computer and checked all the other switches in the main office, she paused by the staircase. Time to face Hugh.

Would she have the nerve to talk to him about the un-finished business between them?

She took a deep breath, headed upstairs and rapped on Hugh's closed door.

'Yes?' he called.

She opened the door and leaned against the door jamb. 'Tarquin said to tell you when I was leaving so you could lock up.'

'OK. Thanks.' He barely glanced at her, concentrating on a file on his desk.

He looked tired, she thought, as if a gazillion things were on his mind and stopping him sleeping. She knew the feeling. He clearly wasn't going to bring up the subject, because he was too stubborn. Which meant that she'd have to be the one who initiated the conversation. She walked over and sat on the edge of his desk. Hugh looked up at her again and glowered. 'What?'

She wasn't fooled by the brusqueness. 'You were in earlier than everyone else, and you're here later than everyone else. It's been like that ever since we got back from Oxfordshire. Carry on like this and you're going to risk burn-out.'

'Thank you for your concern, but my mother doesn't need anyone to help her nag me.'

His tone was snippy enough to make her back off. Except she'd seen that tiny glint of vulnerability in his eyes before he'd looked away. So maybe Grace was right and he was feeling as antsy as she was, and for the same reasons. She knew she was taking a huge risk here and it could all go horribly wrong, but on the other hand if she didn't try then she knew she'd always regret it. She leaned over and stroked the hair back from his forehead. 'Hey,' she said softly.

He looked at her again, and his pupils were huge. So he *did* react to her then.

'You've done enough for today,' she said. 'Come and have dinner with me.'

He was silent for so long that she thought he was going to refuse. She was about to back away and tell him to ignore anything she said because she was sleep-deprived and that meant her mouth wasn't in sync with her brain, when he asked softly, 'Are you asking me out on a date, Bella Faraday?'

His voice was deep. Slightly raspy. Just as he'd sounded when he'd made love with her and whispered her name. And it sent a thrill right the way through her.

'I'm asking you back to my place,' she said. 'There's not going to be anything super-fantastic on the menu, just a stir-fry, because I'm really *not* a very good cook. But it does mean that you won't have to make anything for yourself when you finally leave here and go home.'

He looked at her, wide-eyed with surprise. 'You're mothering me?'

She gave him a rueful smile. 'As you said, your mother doesn't need any help.'

He grimaced. 'Sorry. That was rude and unfair of me.'

'And a defence mechanism. You're snippy when you want people to back off.'

He raised an eyebrow. 'So you're a psychologist as well as an artist, now?'

'Nope. Just someone who also uses a defence mechanism. Except mine's sunshine rather than grumpiness.'

He smiled, then, and rested his hand against her cheek. 'Bella. Go home.'

His touch made heat zing throughout her body. And

maybe short-circuited her brain, because she said, 'Not without you.'

'Bella—I've already told you, I don't do relationships.'

'Neither do I.' She dragged in a breath. 'But you and I, we've been circling each other in the office ever since we went to Oxfordshire. And I think we need to...'

He was staring at her mouth. 'Need to what?'

She twisted her head to one side and pressed a kiss into his palm. 'Talk.'

His pupils dilated even more, making his eyes seem completely black. 'Uh-huh.'

'Maybe among other things,' she admitted. Because talking wasn't all she had in mind. Particularly when he was this close to her.

He moistened his lower lip with the tip of his tongue. 'Do you really think it's a good idea for you and me to be alone in a room that might have a bed nearby?'

She smiled. 'Who needs a bed?'

He groaned. 'Bella, you're killing me.'

'Maybe,' she said, 'we need to get this out of our systems. Unfinished business and all that.'

'I don't do for ever,' he warned.

'Neither do I.' And this time she leaned forward and touched her mouth to his. Really, really lightly. Every nerve-end in her lips tingled.

Was he going to kiss her back? Pull her into his arms and really kiss her? Anticipation danced through her. Any second now. Any second...

Hugh dragged in a breath. 'Bella. Right now, my self-control is hanging by the thinnest thread. We can't do this. Go home.'

It was enough of a confession to give her the courage to ignore his protests. She curled her thumb and fingers into her palm and widened the gap between her first and middle finger, as if her hand were a pair of scissors, then smiled at him and 'snipped'. 'Come home with me,' she said softly.

She could see the struggle in his face. Hugh the honourable man, who wanted to do the right thing and keep his employee at a respectable distance, versus Hugh the lover, who remembered how in tune their bodies had been and wanted to do it all over again.

Then he pulled her into his arms and she knew that the lover had won.

When she surfaced from the kiss, she whispered, 'Ready?'

'Not in a million years.' He kissed her again. 'We need to lock up.'

His head and heart were still warring, she guessed.

She waited for him to lock up, then took his hand.

'My car's outside,' he said.

She nodded, and followed him out to the tiny car park behind the offices. He actually opened the passenger door for her; she loved his old-fashioned good manners.

Then he drove her home and parked outside the road by her flat.

'Do I need a parking permit or anything?' he asked.

Yes, but she didn't want him to have time to think about this and change his mind. 'There won't be any traffic wardens around at this time of night,' she said.

He kissed her. 'I wouldn't bet on that, but OK. You're worth a parking ticket.'

She grimaced. 'Now you've made me feel guilty.'

'Good.' He gave her a slow, sensual smile. 'You can make it up to me.'

He held her hand all the way between the car and her

front door. Once they were inside, he slid his hands into her hair and kissed her until she was dizzy. 'I can't get you out of my head,' he said, holding her close.

'Me, too,' she admitted. She slid her hand under the hem of his T-shirt and splayed her hands against his abdomen. 'Every time I close my eyes, I see you. And I want you, Hugh. It's driving me crazy.'

'Me, too,' he admitted. 'Let's do something about it.'

She took his hand and led him to her room. Slowly, she took off his T-shirt; then she took a step backwards, looked at him and sucked in a breath. 'I want to paint you.'

'Oh, yes?'

'Like Michelangelo's David.'

He grinned. 'I'm hardly a fourteen-foot-tall statue.'

'Scaled down,' she said, grinning back. 'But you're still wearing too much.'

'So are you,' he pointed out.

She spread her hands. 'Do something about it, then.'

He kissed her, then stripped off her T-shirt; and then it was her turn to get rid of his jeans. He followed suit, stroking every inch of skin he uncovered as he removed the soft denim, then making her whimper when he kissed the soft undersides of her breasts and drew a path downwards.

Bella wasn't sure who finished stripping whom, but finally they were naked and in her bed and he was inside her. And the world felt very right indeed.

As they lay curled up together afterwards, her stomach rumbled. 'Sorry,' she said, feeling the heat flare into her cheeks.

He laughed and kissed her. 'It's not just you. Sorry. I was hungrier for you than I was for food.'

'Me, too,' she admitted. 'It's been driving me crazy this last couple of weeks, seeing you in the office and knowing I was supposed to keep my hands off you.'

'That's why I've been skulking in my office instead of coming downstairs with the rest of the team,' he said, and kissed her again. 'Bella, we need to talk. We need to work out how we're going to deal with this.'

'The Vegas principle again?' she asked.

'Maybe,' he said.

'Let's eat, first,' she suggested. 'It might get some brain cells working properly.'

'Good idea.' He climbed out of bed and started to get dressed.

Bella was tempted to tell him not to bother putting his T-shirt back on, but a wave of shyness stopped her; she, too, scrambled out of bed and pulled on her clothes.

'Take a seat,' she said in the main room of her flat, gesturing to the little bistro table in her kitchen area.

'Now I think I know why your desk is so untidy,' he teased.

'Because there's more room on it than there is in my flat?' she asked wryly.

'It's, um, bijou,' he said.

'I like it.'

He stroked her face. 'It's a nice flat.'

'But the whole thing's hardly bigger than the boot room in the house where you grew up.'

'Isn't there a saying that lovely things come in small packages?' he asked. He kissed her lightly. 'Starting with you.'

'Hmm. Sit down and I'll feed you,' she said.

Except when she was making the stir fry, she managed to burn the chicken slightly, and then the noodles caught on the bottom of the wok as well, and the vegetables had somehow gone watery. The whole thing looked disgusting and smelled disgusting—and she dreaded to think what it would taste like. Even a sachet of sweet chilli sauce wouldn't be able to disguise the burned or watery bits.

No way could she serve him this.

'I'm so sorry,' she said, and bit her lip. 'This has all gone a bit wrong. I wish I was more like Gracie—she's a great cook and I've never got the hang of anything more than cupcakes, pancakes and Yorkshire puddings,' she finished miserably.

Hugh came over to her, gave her a hug and kissed her frown away. 'It's no big deal. Actually, I'm an OK cook. Ma taught us all before we left for uni. Do you mind me taking over your kitchen?'

'But I was supposed to cook for you, because you're tired. I can't make you cook for me.'

He kissed the tip of her nose. 'The thought was there, and it's appreciated. But right now you're stressed, and cooking relaxes me anyway. Let me do this for you.'

'OK. And thank you. But I need to get rid of this mess first.' She gestured to the wok.

'Sure.'

She scraped the ruined stir fry into the bin and put the burned pan to soak in the sink. 'Would you like a glass of wine?' she asked.

He shook his head. 'Thanks for the offer, but I'm driving.'

Obviously he wasn't planning to stay the night, then. Well, she shouldn't have expected it. He'd made it very clear that he didn't do relationships. Neither did she, really; so this was just unfinished business to get it out of their systems. 'You'd still be under the limit with one glass,' she pointed out.

'My best friend's wife was killed by a drunk driver, eighteen months ago,' he said softly. 'Since then, none of our group of friends touches a drop of alcohol if we're driving.'

Her eyes widened. 'Oh, poor Tarquin! But I thought he was…' Her voice faded. 'Um. Well.'

'Not Tarquin,' he said. 'His partner—who is indeed male—is just fine. I was talking about Roland. He went to school with Tarq and me. He's a silent partner in Insurgo.' He gave her a sidelong look. 'Though I guess it's a bit greedy, having two best friends.'

Just lucky, Bella thought. She'd been perfectly happy with one—until it had all gone wrong. 'There's nothing wrong with having two best friends,' she said. 'So can I get you a coffee instead?'

'Thanks. That'd be good.'

'I'm afraid it's instant,' she warned. Because Kirk had taken their posh coffee machine as well, and replacing it had been a wee bit out of her budget.

'Instant's fine,' he reassured her.

She made coffee for them both while he rummaged in her cupboards and her fridge. Within ten minutes he'd made the best pasta carbonara she'd ever eaten in her life.

'Is there anything you're not good at?' she asked.

He laughed. 'My ego says thank you.'

'Seriously. You're good at business, you're good at music, you can dance, you're good in b—' She stopped, feeling her face heat. 'Well.'

'Have you gone shy on me, Bella?' His eyes glittered with amusement, but she knew he was laughing with her rather than at her.

'I'm going to shut up and eat my dinner. Which really I should've made for you, except there's no way I could produce anything as excellent as this.'

They ate in silence that wasn't quite companionable but wasn't quite awkward either, then shared a tub of posh ice cream from her freezer.

'I guess,' he said when they'd sorted out the washing up, 'we need to deal with the elephant in the room.'

'You and me.'

'Yeah.' He blew out a breath. 'Bella, I don't do relationships—nothing more than casual, anyway. And I never, ever mix work and relationships.'

'Something obviously happened to make you feel that way,' she said. She'd picked up that much from his family and Tarquin. But would he trust her enough to tell her?

There was a long, long pause. Then he nodded. 'It was a couple of years ago. Insurgo had just hit the big time, and this woman came to the offices to ask if I'd sign her. I said no, because right at that moment my list was full, and she asked me for two minutes to change my mind. And then she sang for me.' He looked away. 'She sang "The First Time Ever I Saw Your Face". She was good. Seriously good. I fell in love with her voice.'

'I love that song,' Bella said. 'There was a version a while back that I really liked—who sang it?' She thought about it. 'Oh, I remember now. Jessie Harrison.'

'That would be her,' Hugh said softly.

'Jessie Harrison? Seriously?' She stared at him. 'But she isn't one of your artists.' Jessie wasn't on the list that Tarquin had given her. Bella would've recognised her name.

'Not any more, she isn't.'

Bella had a nasty feeling where this was going. 'You were dating her?'

'Yes. It happened one night when we were in the studio. She'd been working on a song and couldn't get it right, and she wanted my help.' He paused. 'I played piano for her and did the harmonies, and suggested a few changes to the music—and then somehow I ended up taking her home. A couple of months later, she moved in with me.'

Now Bella was beginning to understand what his brother had been getting at. Obviously the reason why Hugh didn't play the piano or sing in public was because it reminded him of being with Jessie. Working with her, loving her, having his heart broken by her.

Yet he'd sung 'Edelweiss' with Bella, to take the heat off her when their plan to make her his unsuitable girlfriend had gone wrong. And she realised now that it must have brought back memories and hurt him.

'I'm sorry,' she said softly.

'I loved her, and I thought she loved me,' Hugh said, 'but it turned out I was her stepping stone to a bigger label and a bigger career. Six months after she moved in with me, I did something very stupid. Because I was in love with her, I assumed she was just being scatty and hadn't got round to signing her new contract. I'd already put a lot of work into her new album, and I'd put a lot of money into promotional stuff.'

'And it didn't happen?' Bella asked softly.

'It didn't happen,' he confirmed. 'She told me she was leaving Insurgo for another label.'

'What about all the work you'd done—all the things you'd paid out for?'

'It was her word against mine. She hadn't signed anything and I'd gone ahead on an assumption I should never have made. There was nothing I could do except absorb the losses.' He dragged in a breath. 'But it was a really bad business decision that put the label at risk for a while, until Ro decided to invest. I hate that I let everyone down because I let my heart rule my head.'

'I know that feeling,' Bella said. 'It's not much fun.'

'Jessie didn't just leave Insurgo. She left me, too.' He shrugged. 'I found out she'd been having an affair with the head of her new label. That's how, she, um, got him to sign her.'

'That's a really vile way to treat someone.' Bella could understand now why Hugh didn't want to mix work and relationships. He'd been badly burned. But she wasn't Jessie and she would never behave like Jessie had. Surely Hugh could see that?

'I've kind of lost my faith in relationships since then,' he said.

She could appreciate that, too. 'Yeah. It's hard to get your trust back when someone lets you down.'

'That sounds personal.'

She nodded. 'You told me the truth about your past, so I guess I should tell you about mine. Even though it makes me feel so stupid.' She sighed. 'I'd been living with Kirk for six months, though we'd been dating for a year before that. He'd gone all secretive on me for a few weeks. I thought he was going to ask me to marry him, and he was planning this amazing proposal—which was why he was acting oddly, because he wanted it to be a surprise—and I was so happy. I was going to say yes.'

She blew out a breath. 'Except it turned out he'd been seeing my best friend. Instead of proposing to me, he went off with her.'

Hugh winced. 'Your boyfriend and your best friend? That's a double betrayal. Nasty.'

She might as well tell him the worst. Just so he knew how naïve and stupid she'd been. 'He cleared out our bank account as well. Which is why it hit me so badly when my client went bust a couple of months back.' She grimaced. 'Thankfully Grace is an accountant. When I went freelance, she told me that I should always put my tax money to one side in an account I never touched as soon as a client's payment cleared, and to keep a cushion of three months' salary in my bank account. So, although Kirk wiped out my cushion, at least I can still pay my tax bill without worrying where to find the money.'

'But how did he manage to take all the money out of your account?' he asked.

'Online banking—he just transferred all the money to a different account. When you have a joint current account, it seems it doesn't matter how much you each put in to the account; you can both take out however much you like because the bank treats it as jointly owned money,' she explained. 'The bank said if it'd been a savings account, that would've been different and I could've taken him to court for theft. But it was a current account, so I couldn't because he had as much right to the money as I did.' She sighed. 'And how stupid does that make me?'

'Not stupid. Naïve, perhaps,' Hugh said. 'But you loved him and you had no reason not to trust him. Were there any signs that he was going to take all your money?'

'No. He'd been seeing a lot of my best friend, but I thought it was all to do with the secret proposal and that she was helping him plan it. It was the same as you and Jessie, really. You loved her and you had no reason not to trust her, either.' She looked levelly at him. 'You and I—we both made the same kind of mistake, and we both paid for it.'

'Very true.'

'So where does that leave us now?' she asked.

He blew out a breath. 'I'm attracted to you, Bella. Seriously attracted.'

And it was mutual, she thought.

'You're the first person I've really wanted to date since Jessie.'

'And you're the first person I've wanted to date since Kirk.' The first person she'd slept with since Kirk. 'But?' she asked. Because it echoed as loudly in her head as if he'd actually said the word.

'But,' he said softly, 'I learned from my mistakes. I'm never going to mix business and relationships again.'

She narrowed her eyes at him. 'Are you saying, if we start dating then I have to find another job?'

He paused for a long, long time. And then he said, 'Yes.'

She frowned. 'That's totally unreasonable, Hugh. I'm not Jessie, just as you're not Kirk.'

'I know.'

'We can keep it strictly business in the office and see each other outside. There's no reason why we can't separate our relationship from work. We're both grown-ups.'

'You came up to my office tonight and kissed me,' he pointed out.

She blinked. 'So you're saying that this is all my fault?'

He raked a hand through his hair. 'No. Just that it's not negotiable. If we see each other, we can't work together.'

'So I have to choose between seeing you and keeping my job.' She frowned. 'Can you not see how unreasonable that is?'

'Yes,' he said. 'But it doesn't stop me feeling it. I can't keep working with you and seeing you.'

'I admire the fact you have strong principles,' Bella said, 'but actually, right now I think you're being really stubborn and inflexible. You're not taking into account that life doesn't stay the same all the time. Things *change*, Hugh.'

'Not this.'

She stared at him. 'Think about this, then: whatever I decide to do, I lose something. According to your rules, I have to give something up—either you or my job.'

'We can't work together,' he said again.

And he didn't have to give anything up. Admittedly, Insurgo was his company and his last relationship had put it all at risk, so she could understand why he was so antsy about getting involved with someone he worked with. But she was going to be the one making all the sacrifices—which wasn't fair. 'I need time to think about this,' Bella said. 'And I think you, do, too.'

'Yes.' He looked at her, unsmiling. 'So I guess I'll see you tomorrow. Or not.'

Depending on whether she chose him or his job. Or neither, though he hadn't seemed to consider that as an option. Which made her even antsier.

'I guess,' she said.

Unless she could find an argument to convince him

that there was another way. One that didn't involve either of them making a sacrifice. But would he be able to compromise? Or had he been hurt too badly to let himself try again?

CHAPTER NINE

BELLA SAT MISERABLY on the sofa with her knees drawn up and her arms wrapped around her legs for half an hour after Hugh left. Then she pulled herself together and went to splash her face with water.

She needed to think about this—and, better still, to think aloud and work out what to do. Right now there was only one person she knew who'd let her talk and help her see her way through this. She picked up the phone and called her sister. 'Gracie? It's Bella.'

'Are you OK, sweetie?' Grace asked.

'Sure,' Bella fibbed.

'You don't sound it. What's happened?'

Bella sighed. 'I talked to Hugh.'

'I'm coming straight over,' Grace said. 'Hold on. I'll be with you in twenty minutes.'

'You don't have to—' Bella began, but the phone line was already dead.

Twenty minutes later, Grace used her spare key to Bella's flat, walked in and gave her a hug.

'You didn't have to come over,' Bella said.

'I most certainly did,' Grace corrected her. 'You're my little sister, and there's no way I'm letting you cry yourself to sleep.' She hugged Bella. 'Right. Cake and hot chocolate.'

'I don't have any cake,' Bella said miserably.

'I do,' Grace said, and took a wrapped cake from her bag. 'Emergency ginger cake.' While the milk for the hot chocolate was heating in the microwave, Grace cut them both a slice of cake, then finished making the hot drinks and sat down with Bella on the sofa. 'Right. Tell me everything.'

Bella did so, ending with, 'So it seems I have a choice. Either I lose him or I lose my job.'

'Maybe,' Grace said carefully, 'you might be better off without both of them.'

'How do you mean?'

'If you choose the job, it's going to be hard to work with him.'

Bella sighed. 'He's being totally unreasonable about this.'

'Which is why I'm worried,' Grace said. 'Supposing you choose him and you find another job—and then he lets you down?'

'I'm not exactly planning to live with him and open a joint bank account with him,' Bella said dryly.

'OK. You've already told me he's not like Kirk. And, although I wasn't in a fit state to remember much when I met him, you've said he has a good heart and I trust your judgement. So I guess, when it comes down to it, the real question is what do *you* want?' Grace asked.

'I want Hugh,' Bella said. 'But, because he's being stubborn about it, that means losing my job—which I can't afford to do.'

'I've got savings,' Grace said immediately. 'I can cover

your bills. So you don't have to worry about money. Not now and not ever.'

'That's so lovely of you, and I appreciate it,' Bella said, 'but I'm going to say no. Not because I'm an ungrateful, spoiled brat, but because I want to stand on my own two feet. I want to be able to hold my head high, instead of having to rely on you or Mum and Dad to bail me out all the time.' She sighed. 'I want Hugh, but I can't be with someone who's not prepared to even consider meeting me halfway. Having principles is a good thing—something that Kirk didn't have—but Hugh's at the opposite extreme of the spectrum. And if he can't learn to compromise, then we don't stand a chance.' She looked plaintively at her sister. 'Why can't life be simple?'

Grace squeezed her hands. 'I wish I could wave a magic wand for you, Bel.'

'You already have. You came straight over when I called, you brought me cake and you listened.' Bella swallowed hard. 'The only person who can sort this out is me.'

'Together with Hugh.' Grace bit her lip. 'I feel guilty, because I'm the one who told you to talk to him in the first place.'

'No. You were right. We needed to talk.' Bella lifted her chin. 'And now I have to think about it. Long and hard. And then…' She sighed. 'Then I need to make a decision.'

'Sleep on it,' Grace advised. 'And if you want to talk to me about it, even if it's stupid o'clock in the morning and you've just woken up, then just pick up the ph—. No, actually, scratch that,' she corrected. 'You don't need to call me, because I'll be right here. I'll stay with you tonight.'

Bella hugged her. 'I love you. But you really don't

have to stay.' Her bed was only big enough for one and her sofa wasn't big enough to sleep on, which meant that one of them would have an uncomfortable night on the floor. And she knew that Grace would be the one to insist on taking the floor.

'I can sleep on the fl—' Grace began, unconsciously echoing her younger sister's thoughts.

'No, you can't. And, although I can lend you pyjamas and toiletries, my clothes would be totally unsuitable for a day at your office. Not to mention the fact that you're four inches taller than I am, so nothing I own would fit you properly anyway,' Bella pointed out.

'True,' Grace said. 'In that case, go and have a shower and get into your pyjamas. We're going to snuggle up on your sofa under a throw and watch a rerun of *Friends* for a bit.'

Exactly what Bella had done with Grace on the very first day she'd met Hugh—the day when Hugh had rescued them from the Fifty Shades of Beige party. And she was pretty sure her sister remembered that, too. Tears pricked her eyelids. 'Oh, Gracie.'

'It'll work out,' Grace said gently. 'You're strong and you're brave, and you'll make the right decision when you've slept on it.'

Snuggling up with her sister on the sofa—with the help of their favourite comedy, more cake and more hot chocolate—made Bella feel marginally less miserable. But she knew that Grace needed to be up early tomorrow for work and it wasn't fair to keep her up late. Especially as she could see her sister's eyelids drooping.

'Go home, sweetie,' she said. 'You've got work tomorrow.'

Grace shook her head. 'I don't want to leave you.'

'I'll be fine,' Bella reassured her. 'Really. I'm already a lot better than I was.'

'I'll go,' Grace said, 'but only on condition you promise to ring me if you need me. Any time. And I mean *any* time.'

Bella knew she meant it. 'I will, and thanks.'

'And I meant it about covering your bills. Even if you insist on it being a temporary loan,' Grace said. 'If you decide to leave Insurgo, I can help you out until you find another job. It doesn't mean you're stupid or pathetic or needy—it's what sisters do. You had my back when I called off my wedding to Howard. And I've got yours now.'

Bella had to blink back the tears. 'I love you,' she said.

'I love you, too.'

'Text me when you get home.'

Grace laughed. 'You sound as if you're turning into me.'

Good, Bella thought. Maybe Grace's capable, calm togetherness would rub off on her and help her make the right decision.

She didn't sleep much that night. Every time she looked at the clock, the minute hand barely seemed to have moved. The next morning, she felt groggy and her head ached. She washed her hair, drank two big glasses of water and took some paracetamol.

Time to make her decision. Hugh or her job? Whatever she did, she'd lose.

She thought about it for a long time, and eventually came to the conclusion that this was the only way forward. She typed a text to Hugh on her phone, but didn't send it; she needed to bite the bullet, first.

She rang the Insurgo office, hoping that Hugh wouldn't

be the one to answer. She actually crossed her fingers as the call connected and she heard the ringing tone, and then to her relief Tarquin answered.

'Hi, Tarq, it's Bella.'

'You sound terrible,' he said immediately. 'Are you calling in sick?'

'I, um—no, actually.' She sighed. 'I'm, um, afraid I'm resigning. For personal reasons. With immediate effect. Anything of mine in the office, just give to the local charity shop if nobody else wants it.'

'What?' He sounded utterly shocked. 'Bella, sweetie, are you all right? What's happened? Is there anything I can do, anyone I can ring for you?'

His concern and kindness nearly undid her. But she lifted her chin. She needed to do the right thing and stand on her own two feet. 'No, I'm fine.' As fine as you could be with a broken heart. 'I'm sorry to let you down. To let everyone down.'

'Sweetie—I don't know what to say, but I'm worried about you.'

'I'll be fine. Really. And I've loved working at Insurgo. I'm sorry to let you all down.' She'd call the café later, wield her credit card and get them to deliver cake to the team on her behalf to say goodbye. 'I need to go now, Tarq.' Before she let herself down by bursting into tears. 'All the best.'

Once she'd hung up, she pressed the button on her phone to send the text to Hugh.

And then she switched off her phone.

Hugh's phone buzzed as he was walking up the stairs to his office. He checked the screen.

Bella.

His heart skipped a beat. So she'd made her decision?
He flicked into the message.

Am leaving Insurgo

She'd chosen him. Thank God. He closed his eyes
with relief, realising just how much he'd wanted her to
make that choice.

His phone beeped again, and he looked at the screen.
Another message from Bella.

Am leaving Insurgo but I can't be with someone who
gives me impossible ultimatums. I wish it could've been
different. Sorry.

What the hell? But she'd just said...

He looked at the previous message. At the bottom, in
a different script, it said: This message has only been
partially downloaded.

Yeah. And how.

He really hadn't expected this. He'd given her the
choice of a working relationship or a proper relationship. He'd never dreamed that she'd pick a different option: neither.

He was still trying to get his head round it when his
best friend stormed in to his office and slammed the
door behind him.

'What the hell did you do?' Tarquin asked. 'Bella's
resigned and, after the conversation we had with Ro, I
know it's your fault. What did you do?'

'Something very stupid. Don't worry. I'll find you another designer,' Hugh said wearily.

'Not like Bella, you won't. And nobody can believe

she's just left like that. Just what did you do?' Tarquin asked again.

Hugh shook his head. 'You know how I feel about things. I can't mix work and relationships.'

'So you're seeing her?'

That had been the plan. But he'd got that wrong. 'No.'

'Then what the…?' Tarquin shook his head. 'I don't understand what's going on.'

Hugh handed over his phone. 'Here. Read it for yourself.'

Tarquin read the text, then stared at Hugh with narrowed eyes. 'What was the ultimatum?'

'Work and relationships don't mix,' Hugh said.

'You mean you actually asked her to choose between you and Insurgo?'

Hugh winced. 'Put like that, it sounds bad.'

'Sounds bad? It *is* bad, Hugh. Really bad,' Tarquin said. 'I can't believe you did that.'

Hugh was rather beginning to wish that he hadn't, either.

'You,' Tarquin said, 'are my best friend as well as my business partner. Which is why I can tell you that you're also the most stupid, stubborn, *unreasonable* man I've ever met, and right now I don't want to work with you. I don't want to see your face in the office this week. I don't want to speak to you—and, quite frankly, you're lucky the rest of us aren't all walking out on you as well. As of now, you're taking a week's leave.'

Hugh coughed. 'I'm the senior partner.'

'True. But I'm in charge of personnel,' Tarquin reminded him, 'which means that in this case *you* do what *I* say.'

Hugh had never seen his best friend so angry. And he

knew he only had himself to blame. 'I can't take a week off. We've got people in the studio.'

'Most of them are outside bookings. There's only one Insurgo artist due in, and I'll rearrange that for at least a week's time—when your head might be in a fit state to deal with it. I'm not letting you do any more damage this week,' Tarquin said firmly.

'Ouch,' Hugh said, but he knew that he deserved it— and that Tarquin was telling the truth. 'OK. Call me if you need anything.'

'From you? I'll tell you what I need,' Tarquin said. 'I need you to go and have a long, hard think. Look at yourself, look at your life, and think about what you really want. And when you come to your senses and realise that Bella Faraday is the best thing to happen to you—as in the best thing *ever*—you'd better find a fantastic way to apologise to her. And you'd better hope that she's a better person than you are and will actually forgive you. In her shoes, I'm not so sure I would.'

'Noted,' Hugh said dryly.

'Don't you try your Mr Grumpy-in-the-mornings act on me,' Tarquin said, scowling at him. 'Now go home and sort your life out.'

Sorting his life out was easier said than done.

By the time he got back to his house, Hugh was half surprised not to have had a barrage of calls from his family to ask him what he thought he was doing. He was grateful that Tarquin clearly hadn't told his mother or his brothers; though he knew Tarquin had told Roland because his other best friend simply sent him a text saying, You are *such* a moron.

Nothing felt right. Everything felt two-dimensional.

And he knew exactly why: it was because Bella had walked out of his life.

He picked up the phone and called her. A recorded message informed him that her mobile phone was switched off, so please try later or send a text. He tried her landline next, but it went through to voicemail. Which didn't exactly leave him much of an option. Awkwardly, he said, 'Bella, it's Hugh. I'm sorry. I've been a complete idiot. Can we talk? Please call me.'

But she didn't return his call.

He tried both lines again later, several times, with the same result: her mobile was switched off and her landline was switched through to voicemail. Was she avoiding him? Or was she just busy?

Going to her flat in person didn't help, either. Although he rang the bell, there was no answer. He knew Bella wouldn't refuse to answer the door, so clearly she was out. He had no idea where she was and no idea how else to contact her; she was close to her sister, but an internet search to find a phone number for Grace Faraday in London when he couldn't narrow it down to any particular part of the city left him frustrated and grumpy.

It looked as if he'd just have to wait for Bella to contact him. Even though waiting wasn't something that sat well with him.

He paced round the house for a bit, flicked through various television channels without finding anything remotely interesting, and couldn't even lose himself in music. Though he found himself wide awake at three a.m. with music filling his head. He lay there for a bit, trying to ignore it, but the urge was too strong.

In the end, he pulled on a pair of jeans and padded downstairs to his piano. Luckily the houses in his road were well insulated, and he'd installed soundproofing in his music room when he moved in, or the neighbours wouldn't be too happy with him playing the piano at stupid o'clock. He grabbed a manuscript book and a pencil, scribbled down the words in his head, and then started to work out the tune to go with them. By the time it was light again, he'd finished the song.

And he knew exactly what he was going to do.

He showered and changed, though he didn't bother shaving; he just wanted the rest of his life to hurry up and start now. He drove to Bella's and rang the doorbell. There was no answer, but the curtains were still closed— so surely she was there? He rang again and waited, but there was still no answer. Panicking slightly, he leaned on the doorbell.

She opened the door abruptly, rubbing her eyes. 'All right, all right, give a girl time to wake up… Oh,' she said, taking in who was standing on her doorstep.

'I'm sorry. I'm an idiot, please forgive me and—' He broke off, not quite ready to say the three little words yet. 'Come for breakfast.'

'Breakfast?' She blinked, looking confused.

'Breakfast,' he confirmed. 'At my place, and I'm cooking.'

'Hugh, it's the crack of dawn,' she protested.

'It's half past seven,' he pointed out.

'Same thing.'

'No, it isn't. I saw the sun rise this morning, and I'm pretty sure it was about five o'clock.'

She frowned. 'But you're not a morning person. What on earth were you doing up at five o'clock?'

'Finishing.'

'Finishing what?'

'Come for breakfast and I'll show you.'

'Hugh...'

'You don't have to dress up,' he said. 'Just grab some clothes. Please.'

She paused for so long that he thought she was going to say no. But then she gave a weary nod. 'Come in and make yourself a coffee while I have a shower.'

'Thank you.' Though he didn't bother with coffee. He simply paced around her tiny flat, music running through his head. He felt more alive than he'd been in months. Than he'd ever been, if he was honest with himself. And once he'd opened his heart to Bella, told her how he really felt about her, he just hoped she'd give him a second chance.

At last, Bella emerged from the bathroom wearing jeans and a T-shirt. Clearly she'd taken the time to shower, as her hair was damp and not styled, but she hadn't bothered with make-up—and she'd never looked more beautiful to him.

'Ready for this?' he asked softly.

She nodded, and he drove her back to his house. Once he'd made coffee and they'd gone through a stack of pancakes with maple syrup, he said, 'We need to talk.'

'I thought we did all our talking the other night, back at my flat,' she said.

'No, we didn't, because I wasn't thinking straight,' he said. 'I was wrapped in panic because I was so scared of repeating my past mistakes—even though I know you're not Jessie and you'd never behave like her in a million years.' He dragged in a breath. 'I wrote a song for you.'

She looked surprised. 'You wrote a song for me?'

'That's why I was up in the middle of the night. I had music in my head—music you inspired—and...oh, look, why am I blathering on about it? I need you to hear something. That's why I brought you here.'

He led her into his music room and she curled up on his easy chair. Then he sat down on the piano stool and played the song to her.

It was the most beautiful song Bella had ever heard and she knew it came straight from the heart. Hugh's voice kept catching with emotion as he sang, 'You're the missing piece of my heart.'

When the last chord had died away, he turned round to face her. 'I love you, Bella. Yes, I have issues, and I'm probably not going to be the easiest person to share your life with, but I love you and that's not ever going to change. I think I fell in love with you when I saw you bouncing out of Insurgo and into my taxi, that Friday night. I love everything about you—your warmth and your vitality and your brightness. You make my world feel a better place. And I meant everything I sang to you, because you really are the missing piece of my heart,' he said simply.

She simply stared at him. 'I can't believe you wrote this song for me.'

'You took down all the barriers I'd put round myself and set the music free again.' He smiled at her. 'I'm a nicer person when I'm writing music. And you make me a better man.' To Bella's shock, he moved off the piano stool and dropped to one knee in front of her. 'I was totally wrong about not being able to mix business and a relationship. With you by my side, I can do anything; and without you everything just feels wrong. Will you marry me, Bella Faraday?'

She stared at him, not quite sure she was really hearing this. 'But the other night you wanted me to choose between you and my job.'

'Because I was scared. Because I was stupid. But a few hours on my own to think about it and what I could be losing means I've worked through that,' he said. 'I admit, you might still need to tell me I'm stubborn and unreasonable at various points in the future, but I promise I'll listen to you and I'll take it on board—and, more importantly, I'll talk things over with you instead of brooding. So will you give me a second chance? Will you come back to Insurgo?'

'You really think you can work with me?'

'I work a lot better with you than without you. And you're a great designer. Everyone misses you. And they're all pretty mad at me for being an idiot and driving you away,' he admitted.

'So do I still have to choose between you and my job?' she checked.

He shook his head. 'And you took the option I never even considered—not because I'm arrogant but because being without you in any way is so unthinkable. I was wrong, and I'm sorry. Please come back to Insurgo. And—even more importantly—please will you marry me?'

Words she'd expected to hear six months ago from someone else—from a man she'd thought she'd known but she'd been so wrong. So foolish.

And now Hugh—a man she'd known for only a few weeks—was saying those words to her. Offering her for ever. Sweeping her off her feet.

She knew he'd still be grumpy in the mornings. And obstinate. There would be days when he'd drive her crazy.

But, the very first time she'd met him, he'd been there

for her. He'd given her help when she'd needed it, without any strings. And he'd believed in her, been there right by her side when the pretend girlfriend plan had gone wrong.

With Kirk, she'd had dreams. Castles built on sand.

With Hugh, she had reality. Something solid.

'We haven't known each other very long,' he said, as if picking up on her worries, 'but I think you know when you've met the right one. It feels different with you. Like nothing else I've ever known.'

'Me, too,' she whispered.

'And I think that's why I asked you to come home to Oxfordshire with me,' he said. 'Because, even then, I knew you were the right one. The woman who'd just be herself and my family would love her as much as I did— even though I was in major denial at the time.'

'And you let me wear a dress made out of the same curtains your parents had.'

'That's when I knew.' He coughed. 'May I point out that I'm still on one knee, waiting for an answer?'

She leaned over and stroked his face. 'You're not Kirk. You're not going to run off with my best friend and the contents of my bank account. Though you did run off with my heart. Which I guess is why I agreed to go to Oxfordshire with you instead of sending you off with a flea in your ear.' She smiled. 'The answer's yes.'

'To coming back to Insurgo? Or to marrying me?'

'Both,' she said, 'because I love the job—and I love you.'

'I love you, too. So much.' Hugh kissed her, then stood up, scooped her out of the chair, sat down in her place and settled her on his lap. 'One thing. You might have noticed that I'm not very good at waiting.'

'Meaning?' she asked.

'Meaning that I don't want this to be a long engagement.'

'Gracie was engaged to Howard for four years,' she said.

'Way, way, way too long,' he said. 'This is going to be a very short engagement. As short as we can possibly make it.'

'So you're telling me I don't get an engagement party like Nigel and Victoria's—a tea party with your older relatives, a dress made out of curtains and a sneaky dance in the orangery?' she asked.

'How about a wedding in a tiny parish church in Oxfordshire, a party afterwards in my parents' ballroom, and as many sneaky dances as you like in the orangery and a walk in the bluebell woods with the full carpet out?' he countered.

She blinked. 'But the bluebells are out now.'

'And they'll still be out for the next three weeks,' he said softly. 'I reckon we can organise a wedding in three weeks—don't you?'

She grinned. 'I see what you mean about not being good at waiting. Yes, we probably can organise a wedding in three weeks, but we're going to need help.'

'I have a feeling that the Moncrieffs and the Faradays are all going to be very happy if we ask them to help us sort things out,' he said. 'Plus Tarquin and Roland.'

'Hmm. It sounds to me as if we're going to have two best men,' she said.

'Is that OK?' He looked worried.

She kissed him. 'It's very OK. I haven't met Roland yet, but if he's anything like Tarq we'll get on famously. Though, Hugh, if we're working to a deadline of three weeks, we're going to have to start asking people now.'

He grabbed his phone. 'OK. We'll start with a synchronised text to our parents, siblings and best fr—' He stopped. 'Um. Sorry.'

'Don't apologise. You haven't brought back any bad stuff. I do still have a best friend,' Bella said softly, 'but she's usually known to the world as my sister.'

'And I hope also as our chief bridesmaid.' He paused. 'How many bridesmaids can we have? Can we ask my sisters-in-law? Because, um, they all told me you were perfect for me at Nigel and Victoria's engagement.'

'Oh, bless.' Bella smiled. 'Of course. And we need Sophia—she'll be perfect as the flower girl.'

'You are utterly wonderful. And I intend to tell you that every single day. As well as telling you how much I love you.' He typed in a message on his phone.

Bringing Bella to see the bluebells this weekend. Need everyone there for family meeting to plan our wedding.

'How about this?' he asked, and handed the phone to her.

She read it swiftly. 'Perfect. OK.' She handed his phone back and grabbed hers from her pocket. '"Going to see the bluebells at Hugh's parents' in Oxfordshire at weekend. Need you to come with us as is also family meeting to plan our wedding,"' she said as she typed.

'Perfect,' he said.

They both put all the phone numbers in to the right place and smiled at each other. 'Ready?' he asked.

She nodded. 'Go.'

Simultaneously, they pressed Send.

'What do you think—maybe ten seconds before we get a response?' Hugh asked.

'About that,' Bella agreed.

They counted.

On cue, both their phones started ringing and beeping with texts from the people who were obviously trying to call and discovering that the line was engaged.

'And let the wedding planning craziness begin,' Bella said with a grin.

EPILOGUE

Three weeks later

WHEN THEIR PARENTS had gone down to the hotel reception to wait for the other bridesmaids to arrive, Grace turned to Bella. 'Are you absolutely sure about this? Because if you've got even the *slightest* doubt, you walk away now and we'll all support you.'

'I'm absolutely sure,' Bella confirmed. 'Hugh's everything I want.'

'Then I wish you both a lifetime of happiness together,' Grace said softly. 'And you look amazing.'

'So do you. And I can't believe we've organised everything in less than three weeks.'

Grace laughed. 'With Team Faraday and Team Moncrieff joining together—of course we've managed to organise everything in the shortest space of time possible between us!'

'You're all pretty awesome,' Bella agreed.

'And your new in-laws are fantastic,' Grace said. Neither of them said it but both were thinking, the Moncrieffs were so unlike the Suttons, and how nearly Grace had been trapped in a lifetime of misery.

'Thankfully you're not a Bridezilla, so it was relatively easy to sort everything out,' Grace said.

'It's not the dress or the food or even the venue that's the most important bit of a wedding,' Bella said. 'It's the vows and the people there.'

'Totally,' Grace agreed. 'Though I have to admit I'm glad it's the perfect day for an early summer wedding— much better to have bright sunshine than trying to dodge the showers.'

Bella hugged her. 'Sorry. I'm being selfish. This must be so hard for you, considering that right now you should've been just back from your honeymoon.'

'Actually, no,' Grace corrected. 'You're not selfish at all, and today's confirmed for me that I did the right thing. When you and Hugh are together, you both glow— and that's not how it was for Howard and me. I think we both owed it to each other to let ourselves find the person who'd make us light up and who we could light up in return.'

'But you just blinked away tears,' Bella pointed out.

'Those are tears of happiness,' Grace said softly, 'because I'm so glad for you. You've got the kind of love you deserve.'

There was a knock on the hotel room door and their parents came in, followed by Hugh's sisters-in-law and little Sophia, all dressed up in their wedding finery.

'Look at you all—you're gorgeous,' Bella said in delight.

'Bel-Bel,' Sophia cooed, and Bella scooped her up for a kiss.

'My little Sophia.' She grinned. 'We're so going to do "Row, Row, Row Your Boat" later.'

'Bo!' Sophia said happily.

'Careful,' Poppy said, 'or she'll have us all singing that down the aisle.'

'What an excellent idea.' Bella laughed. 'So are we all ready to get this show on the road?'

'We certainly are,' Harriet said. 'Even though we still can't quite believe how fast this is all happening.'

'Sorry. I did kind of steal your and Nigel's thunder, Victoria,' Bella said.

'No, you didn't. It's good to see Hugh happy,' Victoria said. 'And it could be worse. You could've made us all wear bridesmaid dresses made out of curtains.'

In response, Poppy started singing 'Do Re Mi', and everyone joined in, ending in gales of laughter.

Finally it was time to go downstairs, where the bridal cars were waiting to take everyone to the tiny country church where Hugh and Bella were getting married— the church where Hugh's parents had been married and Hugh himself had been christened.

'I'm not even going to ask you if you're sure about this,' Bella's father said when they were in the car. 'Apart from the fact that I know Gracie's already asked you, I can see it in your eyes. Hugh's the right one for you.'

'Absolutely yes,' Bella said.

'Will you please stop checking your watch, sweet-cheeks?' Tarquin asked in exasperation. 'She'll be here. She might be a couple of minutes late, because it's tra-ditional, but she'll be here.'

'She loves you to bits,' Roland added.

'I know. I'm just antsy.' Hugh dragged in a breath. Standing here by the altar, waiting, was much more nerve-racking than he'd anticipated. He'd been there before as Roland's best man, but being the groom gave you a totally different perspective. The ancient Cotswold stone church was full to bursting, there were flowers everywhere he looked, and the sun was shining through the stained glass in the windows, spilling pools of colour over the congregation. Everything was perfect.

Or it would be, when Bella was here.

And then a memory surfaced that made him even more antsy. 'Did I ever tell you, her sister cancelled her wedding three weeks before the big day?'

'And you've had three weeks to organise yours,' Tarquin said. 'But, from what Bella told me, Grace would've been donning a ball and chain instead of a wedding ring, and she did absolutely the right thing in calling it off.'

'Even so, cancelling it just three weeks before the actual day—surely she must've known earlier that she didn't want to get married?' Roland said with a frown. 'She sounds a bit princessy to me. Obviously she's nothing like her sister.'

'Grace is all right, actually—but she is pretty much the opposite of Bella,' Tarquin agreed.

'You would've met her and found out for yourself if you hadn't been off on a conference when the rest of us were doing wedding organising stuff,' Hugh pointed out mildly.

Roland rolled his eyes. 'If you will insist on getting married with practically no notice, Moncrieff...'

'We wanted the rest of our lives to start as soon as possible,' Hugh said softly. 'There was no reason to wait.'

'Hang on. You're not...?' Tarquin asked.

'Expecting a baby?' Hugh finished. 'No. We just didn't want to wait. Because we're sure this is the right thing for us.'

'I remember that feeling,' Roland said softly.

Hugh patted his shoulder. 'I know. And I'm sorry.'

'Don't be sorry. It was the best day of my life. Just as this will be yours,' Roland said.

Suddenly, the organ music changed from Bach to the processional music from *The Sound of Music*.

'So very Bella to choose this one to walk down the aisle to,' Tarquin said with a grin. Then he looked over his shoulder. 'Oh, my. Ro. Look.'

Roland looked. 'Hugh, you definitely need two best men, one either side—because otherwise your knees are going to go weak and you'll fall flat on your face when you turn round and see her. She looks incredible.'

Fortified by their warnings, Hugh looked round to see Bella walking down the aisle towards him on her father's arm. She looked absolutely amazing. Being Bella, she'd made a few alterations to the traditional wedding gown. Her dress was in cream silk and chiffon, with a strapless sweetheart neckline and a ballerina-type skirt which came to just above her ankles and showcased her strappy high heels—which were exactly the same dark red as the bouquet of sunflowers she was holding, the bridesmaids' dresses and the waistcoats and cravats of the men in the wedding party. He knew that Grace had talked her out of dyeing her hair the same colour as the sunflowers, but today she'd gone back to being platinum blonde. Just like the first day he'd seen her.

And she looked like an angel.

'I love you,' Hugh mouthed at her as she joined him at the altar, and was rewarded with a smile that felt as if it lit up the whole church.

They both pledged to love, honour and cherish each other, in front of a whole church full of family and friends. And then came the bit he'd been waiting for. The moment when he could kiss his beautiful bride.

Signing the register and walking back down the aisle as man and wife passed in a blur, and then they were walking on the path outside the church with dried white delphinium petals raining down on them. Hugh's face was aching, but he didn't care because he couldn't stop smiling. Even posing for endless photographs, both at the church and back at his parents' home under the wisteria, didn't try his patience: Roland had been absolutely right, he thought, because this was really the happiest day of his life.

'Libby, Oliver, this is so perfect—thank you so much,' Bella said, hugging them both inside the marquee on the lawn in the back garden.

'It was a team effort between the Moncrieffs and the Faradays,' Oliver said. 'The men put up the marquee and the women did the flowers and the table arrangements.'

'And what gorgeous flowers,' Bella said happily. There were alternating arrangements of red and yellow sunflowers in the centre of the table.

'Come and see the cake,' Hugh said. 'Victoria says the top tier is red velvet, the middle one's vanilla and the bottom one's chocolate.'

In keeping with the rest of the theme, red sunflowers made from fondant icing spilled down the side of the cake in a cascade. 'Just brilliant,' Bella said. 'We're so lucky, Hugh. We have the best joint family in the entire world.'

'We do indeed,' Hugh said.

The meal was perfect, too, and Roland and Tarquin did the perfect double act for the best man's speech, teasing Bella about her ever-changing hair colour and Hugh about having to learn to be less grumpy in the morning now he was married. Oliver welcomed Bella to the Moncrieff family. 'Though I still have to stop myself calling her Maria,' he teased at the end, 'and I'm going to have to check the curtains for cut-outs before she and Hugh leave tonight.'

Bella laughed and raised a glass to him. 'I promise— no scissors, so your curtains are safe. For today, at least!'

Ed welcomed Hugh to the Faraday family. And Hugh's own speech was simple but heartfelt. 'I do enough talking in my day job, so I just want to say that Bella's made me the happiest man alive and I intend to make her the happiest woman alive, I'm glad you're all here to celebrate with us, and I hope everyone else has as happy a day as we're having.'

After the speeches were over and the cake had been cut, the party moved to the ballroom for the dancing. Oliver and Libby had decorated the room with fairy lights, so it looked completely romantic and utterly gorgeous.

Hugh took Bella's hand. 'You know we don't always do things the traditional way,' he said, 'and the first dance is no exception—because we're not actually going to dance to the first song. We also know most of you are pretty sure we're going to use "Edelweiss" or something else from *The Sound of Music* as "our song", because of the first time a lot of you met Bella in this very room. But instead,' he said, 'it's this.' He sat down at the baby grand piano, pulling Bella onto his lap, and began to play the song he'd written for her—'The Missing Piece of My Heart'.

She joined him when he sang the chorus.

And there wasn't a dry eye in the house when they'd finished.

'That's our song,' Hugh said softly. 'The one Bella

inspired. Because she really is the missing piece of my heart. Now, please, I want you all to dance and drink champagne and enjoy yourselves—because today's all about celebrating.'

'Today and the rest of our lives,' Bella said softly.

'The rest of our lives,' Hugh echoed.

* * * * *

Kate Hardy's glamorous new duet
BILLIONAIRES OF LONDON
continues next month, April 2016, with
HOLIDAY WITH THE BEST MAN,
only in Harlequin Romance.
Don't miss it!

MILLS & BOON®
Hardback – March 2016

ROMANCE

The Italian's Ruthless Seduction	Miranda Lee
Awakened by Her Desert Captor	Abby Green
A Forbidden Temptation	Anne Mather
A Vow to Secure His Legacy	Annie West
Carrying the King's Pride	Jennifer Hayward
Bound to the Tuscan Billionaire	Susan Stephens
Required to Wear the Tycoon's Ring	Maggie Cox
The Secret That Shocked De Santis	Natalie Anderson
The Greek's Ready-Made Wife	Jennifer Faye
Crown Prince's Chosen Bride	Kandy Shepherd
Billionaire, Boss...Bridegroom?	Kate Hardy
Married for their Miracle Baby	Soraya Lane
The Socialite's Secret	Carol Marinelli
London's Most Eligible Doctor	Annie O'Neil
Saving Maddie's Baby	Marion Lennox
A Sheikh to Capture Her Heart	Meredith Webber
Breaking All Their Rules	Sue MacKay
One Life-Changing Night	Louisa Heaton
The CEO's Unexpected Child	Andrea Laurence
Snowbound with the Boss	Maureen Child

MILLS & BOON®
Large Print – March 2016

ROMANCE

HISTORICAL

MEDICAL

MILLS & BOON®
Hardback – April 2016

ROMANCE

MILLS & BOON®
Large Print – April 2016

ROMANCE

The Price of His Redemption	Carol Marinelli
Back in the Brazilian's Bed	Susan Stephens
The Innocent's Sinful Craving	Sara Craven
Brunetti's Secret Son	Maya Blake
Talos Claims His Virgin	Michelle Smart
Destined for the Desert King	Kate Walker
Ravensdale's Defiant Captive	Melanie Milburne
The Best Man & The Wedding Planner	Teresa Carpenter
Proposal at the Winter Ball	Jessica Gilmore
Bodyguard...to Bridegroom?	Nikki Logan
Christmas Kisses with Her Boss	Nina Milne

HISTORICAL

His Christmas Countess	Louise Allen
The Captain's Christmas Bride	Annie Burrows
Lord Lansbury's Christmas Wedding	Helen Dickson
Warrior of Fire	Michelle Willingham
Lady Rowena's Ruin	Carol Townend

MEDICAL

The Baby of Their Dreams	Carol Marinelli
Falling for Her Reluctant Sheikh	Amalie Berlin
Hot-Shot Doc, Secret Dad	Lynne Marshall
Father for Her Newborn Baby	Lynne Marshall
His Little Christmas Miracle	Emily Forbes
Safe in the Surgeon's Arms	Molly Evans